MW00461261

"Word has it you want to marry me."

"You appear to be misinformed, Miss Diamond." And while her eyes shot wide and were fixed to his, to set her straight, Holt added coolly, "I never at any time stated that I *wanted* to marry you."

"But you told my father...." Verity began rapidly only for her voice to fade in sudden confusion.

"My recollection of what I told your father was not that I wanted to marry you, but that I *would* marry you."

"My father said you were an honorable man," she said, unable to keep the edge from her voice. "But you would agree to marry me—obviously against your natural inclinations—just because it *appears* you've compromised me while a guest in his home?"

"That—plus a few other reasons."

Books by Jessica Steele

HARLEQUIN ROMANCE

HARLEQUIN PRESENTS

These books may be available at your local bookseller.

Don't miss any of our special offers. Write to us at the following address for information on our newest releases.

Harlequin Reader Service
P.O. Box 52040, Phoenix, AZ 85072-2040
Canadian address: P.O. Box 2800, Postal Station A,
5170 Yonge St., Willowdale, Ont. M2N 6J3

No Honourable Compromise

Jessica Steele

Harlequin Books

TORONTO • NEW YORK • LONDON
AMSTERDAM • PARIS • SYDNEY • HAMBURG
STOCKHOLM • ATHENS • TOKYO • MILAN

Original hardcover edition published in 1984
by Mills & Boon Limited

ISBN 0-373-02687-0

Harlequin Romance first edition April 1985

Copyright © 1984 by Jessica Steele.
Philippine copyright 1984. Australian copyright 1984.
All rights reserved. Except for use in any review, the reproduction or utilization
of this work in whole or in part in any form by any electronic, mechanical
or other means, now known or hereafter invented, including xerography,
photocopying and recording, or in any information storage or retrieval system,
is forbidden without the permission of the publisher, Harlequin Enterprises
Limited, 225 Duncan Mill Road, Don Mills, Ontario, Canada M3B 3K9. All the
characters in this book have no existence outside the imagination of the
author and have no relation whatsoever to anyone bearing the same name
or names. They are not even distantly inspired by any individual known
or unknown to the author, and all the incidents are pure invention.

The Harlequin trademarks, consisting of the words HARLEQUIN ROMANCE
and the portrayal of a Harlequin, are trademarks of Harlequin Enterprises
Limited; the portrayal of a Harlequin is registered in the United States Patent
and Trademark Office and in the Canada Trade Marks Office.

Printed in U.S.A.

CHAPTER ONE

A FROWN touched Verity Diamond's usually un-troubled brow. Her thoughts were again on how vague her father became whenever she mentioned taking up her seat on the board.

Not that she had mentioned it this past month. She appreciated that running a firm as successful as Diamond Small Tools meant he had a lot on his mind, which was why she had decided to be patient, and to wait until he spoke first. But she had celebrated her twenty-first birthday over a week ago now, and *still* nothing had been said!

The ringing of the telephone interrupted her reflections on how, three years ago, her father had concreted her assumption that she would ultimately take her rightful place in the company. And when Mrs Trueman, their housekeeper, left it to Verity to take the call—daytime phone calls to Birchwood House were usually for her anyway—she went to pick up the receiver, and had her more normal sunny humour restored to hear her closest girl friend, Miranda Beddowes, calling to hope that her head was clearer than her own that morning.

'Did I have a good time last night?' Miranda enquired.

'We all did, I think,' Verity replied with a chuckle. 'Though some of us were more able to drive than others.'

'Perhaps if, like you, I made it a rule to always drive myself rather than rely on one of the gang to see me home, it might stop me having that last drink,' opined Miranda.

'You don't always go over the top,' Verity said truthfully, since it was only occasionally that Miranda ended up legless.

'I think I'll keep to leaving my car at home in the evenings,' decided Miranda. 'What I actually rang for was to ask if I'm going to a party tonight. There's a whisper of memory in my head of my agreeing to go somewhere—but where?'

'It's Rollo Hodgson's,' Verity filled in for her. 'His parents are away at the moment—he's celebrating the event.'

They both laughed and spent a few moments discussing the fate of poor Rollo who, although he came from the same wealthy background as the rest of their crowd, unlike the rest of them, had parents who kept him on a short rein. Though, remembering the times she herself had been brought up short by her own parent after some scrape or other, Verity wondered if it was just that Rollo spoke more freely of the wiggings he received than the rest of them.

'Talking of parents,' went on Miranda, 'has your father said anything yet?'

With Miranda, her closest friend, Verity had confided her puzzlement that her father's birthday gift, though absolutely splendid in the shape of a pearl choker, had not included some comic note that said 'Welcome aboard'.

'Not yet,' she replied. And making up her mind on that instant, 'That's why I'm staying in tonight.' A smile was in her voice as she added, 'I think it's high time I had a few words with Himself.'

'Aren't you coming to Rollo's party!'

'Once we get started, my father will want to discuss with me my role in the firm,' Verity excused.

'But can't you come on afterwards? We'll be going

on until bacon and egg time, I expect.'

'I want my father to see how seriously I intend to take my responsibilities,' she declined. 'He—er—wasn't very pleased about that last scrape I got into.'

'Which one was that?' questioned her friend.

'There haven't been that many—not just lately,' said Verity, proud of her unblemished record since her father had cut up rough on that morning, some months back, when she'd told him about the police raid that had ended the one and only visit she and her friends had made to an unlicensed casino the night before.

'Oh, do come tonight,' pressed Miranda. 'Jolyon, for one, will be devastated if you aren't there.'

As far as Verity was concerned, Jolyon Robey could be devastated. If she was to be honest—and she had a true core of honesty in her—having turned down Jolyon's marriage proposal, she was getting just a wee bit tired that he had not accepted that she was just not interested, and that he was still sticking to her side like some limpet.

But Jolyon Robey was soon forgotten when she came away from the phone. Though with her thoughts taken up with her decision to have a serious talk with her father that night, there were many hours to be got through before he came home. Many hours in which she could recall how over the years she had grown up knowing she was not to be discriminated against because she had been born a girl. A boy, it went without saying, would automatically have had a right, like her dreadful cousin Basil, to a seat on the board in due course. She had always known that her father would not deny her that same right.

But it had not been until she had reached the age of eighteen that her father had come right out and given her that promise for when she was twenty-one.

She recalled the occasion vividly. Thinking it unfair

to leave him since he had been both mother and father to her from the time, when she was seven, that her mother had died, she had turned down the chance to go to university. But when she was eighteen, her education finished with, she had asked for a job at the firm, prepared then to do any job, he had told her that there was not a vacancy in any department just then.

He had been honest with her as he always was, when he had explained that though he could manufacture a vacancy for her, having more cause than anyone else to know she had a lively mind and that she thrived on activity, he was reluctant to have her bored from not having enough to do.

Verity had guessed then when, unable to smile, she had striven to hide her disappointment, the her penchant for getting into mischief in the past when things were a bit quiet had gone against her. But, as honest as her father, she had faced that perhaps she had been a teeny bit wild now and then.

But joy had been hers, her disappointment shortlived when, attempting to prise a smile from her, he had gone on to say that when she was twenty-one he would welcome her on to the board.

She had tried her best over the next three years to show him that her days of getting into mischief were over. Though, try as she might, it seemed impossible to avoid the occasional blotting of her copybook—the worst time had been when, in a temper, she had written off her car. Though her father's fury with her when he had threatened to withhold that seat until she could behave more responsibly had taken from her what she had been in a temper about. But she had really scared him then, and herself not a little, although she had walked away from the wreckage without a scratch, and he had ranted at her at some length, refusing to accept her excuse that no one could have foreseen black ice on that patch of road, by bellowing that if she hadn't raced off full throttle in her temper, she would have been going slow enough to have avoided ending up in a ditch.

His threat to withhold that seat on the board had shaken her more than the car smash, even if she had known deep down that he didn't really mean it. But she had buckled down then to reading all she could about what happened at board meetings, and although she had found it enormously confusing she had tried to learn all she could about what happened in a toolroom. And she had even taken a course in business studies. Which should, she thought, have impressed her parent by how she meant to be a very responsible member of Diamond Small Tools.

But, having thought of little else all day, when Clement Diamond came home that evening, Verity held back on the almost overwhelming urge to have her serious talk with him straight away, although he was not looking so strained now as he had been looking a week or two ago.

'Can I get you a drink?' she asked brightly, knowing he was not averse to a tot sometimes if he'd had a sticky day.

'I'd prefer a cup of tea,' he returned, his reply pleasing her, because if his day had been stress-free, then she felt he would be quite up to discussing at length her new role in the firm.

'I'll go and make you one,' she volunteered, excitement bringing a sparkle to her beautiful brown eyes, as over her shoulder as she headed towards the kitchen, she remarked, 'I expect Trudy is up to her eyes getting dinner started.'

But not long after, up in her room, the excitement she had felt because there was nothing to prevent them having that long discussion tonight had taken a dip.

Aware that her father did not care for her to wear trousers at the dinner table, to please him she opted to put on a dress, but all the time, as she changed, anxiety was to ferret at her that he had left it to her to bring the matter up.

Perhaps he had just been testing her to see how keen she was, she worried when, her long black hair neatly brushed, she was ready to go down. But on leaving her room the answer she had found did not sit satisfactorily with her. He had never thought to test her before! And, for heaven's sake, he just knew, without any kind of test being necessary, how much that seat on the board of his company meant to her!

'You're *in* to dinner tonight!' Clement Diamond exclaimed in mock surprise when she joined him, his bushy eyebrows shooting up above the rim of his spectacles.

Anxiety dropped away from her at his obvious good humour. 'I was in to dinner . . .' she paused, not remembering quite when recently she had stayed home, '. . . the other night,' she finished, and had to grin when he pulled a comic face.

Dinner was a happy meal, with Verity, for no reason she could understand, other than some odd instinct, holding back on what she had to ask.

But when Mrs Trueman—Trudy only to Verity but special to them, being more friend than housekeeper, she had been with them so long—came in with the last course and asked her employer if he would be in for coffee, that unaccustomed anxiety was sharp in Verity again. And before he could make any reply, she had butted in to exclaim:

'You're not going out!'

'One rule for you, and another for me?' he answered. But when Trudy, with a resigned look, went out, as Clement Diamond caught his daughter's tense expression, all sign of banter went from him. And, as his eyes slid away from her, he too appeared tense. Then, as if he had made up his mind about something—something which had to be faced—he enquired quietly, 'Any particular reason why you should want me to stay in, Verity?'

Inexplicably she felt the air to be all at once charged. It made her nervous suddenly. Yet she knew she had no need to be nervous of anything. But, as she recalled how over the years her eventual place in the firm had been cut and dried, her plentiful supply of confidence returned. And a grin parted her mouth, showing her perfect even teeth, as she teased:

'Well, it did occur to me that since I'm to be present at the next board meeting of that terrific firm known world-wide for its quality of product, I might get the chairman to fill me in on what's expected of me.'

A small frown of puzzlement touched her brow when he again looked away from her. And all of a sudden, as her confidence began to slip, Verity found she was having the hardest work in the world to keep her grin in place.

'Is—is something the matter?' she was forced to ask when, his expression graver than she could ever remember, he had not replied to her teasing. 'Don't you . . .' Appalled at the sudden, never-thought-of-before question that jumped into her head, Verity had to ask, 'Don't you—want me on the board?' a hoarse note entering her voice as her father returned his eyes to her.

'It isn't that I—don't want you on the board . . .' he began.

'Thank goodness for that!' Verity rushed in on a relieved breath. 'For a minute there . . .'

Promptly she had broken off. Something in her parent's still grave expression was warning her that although he wanted her on his board, there seemed a touch of doubt in his mind somewhere. But her confidence was surging anew when, aware of the times in the past when he had been decidedly stuffy about some of her misdemeanours, she hastened to tell him:

'If you're worried that I shan't take the job seriously, then you have no cause, I promise you.' And to let him see that she was not unaware of her faults, 'I know I've been a bit of a—a rebel, and that I've caused you a few—er—moments of disquiet in the past. But you must have seen, when I stuck at that course in business studies and came away with my diploma, how seriously I intend to take my position.' For added weight, she thought to mention, 'And I haven't put a foot wrong for months now, and . . .' Sharply she was cut off.

'Stop it, Verity!' Clement Diamond ordered. But when she stared at him, he seemed more as though he was struggling for words at her trying to show him how responsible she intended to be than as if he was irritated with her that she was pleading her cause.

Wondering why she should think of it as pleading her cause when, with that seat promised to her, there was no cause to plead, all at once as she looked at him and saw that he was now showing signs of that strain that had not been there when he had first come home, Verity felt tension again.

'What's wrong?' she asked, trying to ignore a sudden instinct that said that something was wrong, very, very wrong, as part of her could not believe that anything could be wrong—how could it be?

'I should have told you before,' he mumbled.

'What, Father?' she pressed, instinct battling against her certain knowledge that her seat on the board was safe. 'What should you have . . .'

'There is no seat on the board available for you,' he cut in swiftly, to shock her so deeply that for ageless moments she just stared at him in stunned silence.

But when, as aware as he that the retirement of his brother had left a seat vacant, she was to recall how her father was capable of keeping a straight face when it suited him, and how he had once play-acted for a week that she was not going to have something which she had set her heart on, Verity was to come bouncing back from the terrible shock he had just given her. She was certain then, for all he had never looked more serious, that he was just teasing her.

'Pull the other one, Clem,' she said saucily, her smile coming out again as she in turn teased him. 'You must have forgotten that I'm fully aware that Uncle Walter retired at Christmas, and that purposely no one else has been appointed so that I should . . .'

'Someone else *has* been appointed,' he interrupted her again. And seeming then to want it all said and out of the way, 'I'm sorry, Verity,' he went on quickly. 'Don't think I don't know how much it would have meant to you. But it's done. The seat you thought was yours has gone, and there won't be another vacancy for . . .'

'*Gone!*' Shaken rigid, her brown eyes wide with shock, she was all set to argue, to yell, and scream even.

'I'm sorry,' he said again, and looked as though he really meant it. 'I should have told you before. I should have done, but . . .'

'It's a joke, isn't it?' she asked, having surfaced a little way from fresh shock to realise that he just couldn't be serious.

But serious he was, when, not backing away from owning his part in any of it, he told her: 'This is no joke, Verity. As chairman of the company, I thought, and the other board members thought with me, that . . .' he hesitated, then went on, '. . . that an outsider might be of more . . .' again he hestitated, '. . . er— benefit to the company. And . . .'

'An outsider!' Verity exclaimed, not believing any of this, 'But you've only ever wanted members of the family at the head. There's never been anyone but a Diamond on that board since you started the company,' she protested.

'One very good reason for letting an outsider in,' he replied, which made no sense to her whatsoever, and had her arguing her case hotly as in the next half hour she was made to see that in the instance of her wanting that seat above all else, her father was not going to give in to her.

That half hour was the worst half hour of her life. Mrs Trueman had come in with a tray of coffee, but had soon gone out again when she heard their voices raised in argument as it slowly sank in on Verity that all her hopes and dreams—she had even thought that one day, if she worked hard, she might be chairman herself—had been snatched away from her by some outsider.

'Who is he?' she asked in hurt, frustrated anger, when that half hour had gone by and her father was still sticking as stubbornly to his guns as she had stuck to hers. 'Who is this outsider? It *is* a man, I suppose?'

His nod did not make her feel any better. Though be it a man or a woman who had done her out of her promised place, she didn't think it would make any difference to the bitter taste of disappointment which she was being forced to swallow.

'You'll have heard his name,' Clement Diamond answered. 'Though to my knowledge you've never met Holt Jepherson. He . . .'

'You've no need to tell me who he is,' she cut in moodily. He was right, she had never met the man— nor did she want to. But she had heard his name mentioned countless times. Around this very dinner table, on those occasions when business associates were invited to dine or spend the weekend, she had heard the name of the tycoon Holt Jepherson. 'I should have thought Diamond Small Tools was small beer after what he's used to,' she said disagreeably. 'Or is he after your job as well as mine?'

'He's content with a seat on the board,' her father replied. And he might have said more, only Verity had suffered a severe blow to her hopes, and she was in no mind to try and hide it.

'Not for long, I'll bet,' she said surlily. 'Hasn't he just pulled off a coup with some other unsuspecting firm?' The details escaped her, but she was sure she could remember hearing how Holt Jepherson had calmly walked in somewhere and had pulled the rug from under some other hopeful company.

'One of his concerns recently took over another company under the noses of the people tipped to get it,' Clement Diamond agreed. 'But it was all very much above board, and,' he smiled as he tried to coax an answering smile from his, in this instance, antagonistic daughter, 'I can assure you he had no wish whatsoever to head Diamond Small Tools. He's a man I could trust with my most valued possession,' he thought to add.

'It would appear that you're living in the same cloud cuckoo land I was living in,' said Verity, seeing nothing at all to smile at. She had argued her point of view and would still be arguing now if she thought it would have done any good. But she knew her father of old, and while for most of the time he let her get away with murder, and could most of the time be sweet-talked out of some stand or other he had taken with her, there had been a few occasions when he had stood firm, when there had been no getting around him. This, she had been made to realise, was one of those occasions.

He had not liked her last remark, she could see that when his smile disappeared and he frowned. Though maybe because he was aware of the greatness of her disappointment, he did not take her to task for her insolence, but instead he said:

'I know you're upset, Verity. But look on the bright side. You . . .'

'Bright side!' she exclaimed, getting angrily to her feet, 'What bright side is there? You *promised* me that seat, but you don't care enough about me to think about that promise twice before offering what's mine to that—that *usurper*, who must already be on more boards than he has time for!'

Anger took her racing up to her room, tears stinging her eyes, but tears, as she snatched up her shoulder bag, which she had no intention of allowing her father to see.

Without any idea of where she intended to go, she was already diving into her bag for her car keys as she left her room and raced down the stairs again.

But, as she darted across the hall to the front door, so her father's voice halted her, that stern note there she respected even if she wasn't liking him very much at that moment, when he demanded to know where she was going.

'Not to paint the village hall shocking pink,' she mumbled uncivilly.

'Nor anywhere else if you're intending to drive yourself,' he told her, suddenly coming on the crusty parent, and causing her to know that despite what she had said, he did care for her very much in that he had never forgotten that she had been in a fury that time she had skidded on black ice and had written off her car.

His concern for her almost had her weakening, and nearly brought her to the brink of apologising for being rude to him. But the blow he had dealt her was too new. And so it was that without saying another word, she dropped her car keys down on the hall table, and with her expression mutinous, went out through the front door.

The long walk she took that night, though effective in cooling her temper, did nothing to lessen the mutiny of her disappointment. And three days later, when she had never been one to stay bad friends with her father for very long, a stubbornness in her character that he could break his promise and deliver such a bombshell, gave her very little to say to him.

But, while loving her father, if not liking him very much just then, Verity was positively hating Holt Jepherson that, when he just didn't need another seat on any board, he had calmly come in and stolen her place.

Never a girl to do anything by halves, when Jolyon Robey telephoned her on the fourth day after her row with her father, Verity's hate for Holt Jepherson still mighty, she was just right to take on any madcap idea. Though since all Jolyon offered was a cosy dinner for two that evening, she did not think much of the idea.

'There's a new club opened down the road from where I live,' she told him, omitting to mention that her father hadn't been at all pleased that planning permission for a Country Club had been granted within a mile of his boundary and that he had done all he could to stop the building going ahead, but fully aware he would think she was letting the side down if she so much as set one foot inside its diabolical portals. 'Why not round up a few of the others?' she suggested. 'It's about time we tried something new.'

'But I thought just you and . . .'

With her eyes going heavenward, Verity cut him off. And since Jolyon hadn't yet got the message, though not wanting to hurt his feelings, she repeated what she had told him a few times before, which all boiled down to the fact that if he wanted to see her that it would have to be with the rest of the crowd.

When he rang off to dial Adrian Lovatt and Rollo Hodgson, she did some dialling of her own. Within half an hour a six-some had been arranged for that night, with Verity opting to meet Sadie Knowles, who was chauffeuring Miranda, in the bar of the new Country Club where Jolyon, Adrian and Rollo would be waiting.

Any compunction Verity felt about going against her father's unspoken wishes when, dressed in green velvet pants and a shimmering top, she bumped into him just coming in as she went out, was lost in the thought that had she been allowed to work at Diamond Small Tools, maybe they would have been coming home together.

'Been working late?' she offered casually in passing.

'Where are you off to?' he asked in reply.

Verity's car was already parked on the drive. She opened the driver's door. 'To liven up the Lower Bassett Country Club,' she replied, unblinking.

The slam of the front door as her father stormed in told her that he was not well pleased.

Compunction was to hit her before she was halfway down the drive. And tears she didn't want stung her eyes. She knew she was behaving abominably, but he had hurt her, and when she was hurt, there was just something in her nature that wouldn't let go, even if she did end up being the one to suffer for it.

Anyway, since it was her idea to go to the wretched Country Club, she was committed now. Especially when she saw, as she recognised from Sadie's car and Jolyon's car, that the others had already arrived.

In no time, given that being a non-member of the

Club meant she had to bat her over-long eyelashes a little to get past the official at the door, Verity was soon part and parcel of the six-some, with much merriment ensuing because the three males of the party had had to pay the full membership fee before they were allowed in. The atmosphere for an hysterical evening was set before they left the bar to go through to where a dinner-dance was taking place.

With the ease of old friends there was much wisecracking and laughter, the noisy six having a whale of a time as, conversation constant, they took in their new surroundings and between courses, tested the floor.

Verity was unperturbed by the occasional look she caught being thrown to her and her companions from other diners, and chimed in with her two-pennyworth as often as the others.

Though she had to admit to feeling a shade uncomfortable when Rollo, with no need to try and impress any of them with his knowledge, aggressively went for the waiter after tasting a sample from the third bottle of wine, and loudly told him that it was unfit for human consumption.

Luckily Adrian stepped in to flatten him by taking a sip, and declaring that there was nothing wrong with it, Adrian, like Verity, going steadier than the others on his intake. But it had been an unpleasant few minutes, though it was probably because of that small dampener, Rollo suddenly remembering his father and the hell he would create if they got slung out and he got to hear of it, that they sobered down for a short while—but not for long. For with talk returning to how the men had had to pay and become members before they were allowed in, laughter started up again.

But while the others went on to be more outrageous, Verity found that she was the only one who didn't feel like collapsing with laughter at Adrian's disgusted comment of, 'Talk about equality of the sexes!'

With them in body if not in spirit, suddenly any pleasure she had been feeling in the evening fell away. Had she been born a boy, then it was for sure no outsider would have had a chance of coming in and robbing her of her place. Her cousin, frightful, spiteful Basil, she called him, had been a board member for some years now.

Her hate for the 'outsider' taking possession of her, Verity had been deep in thought when she was snapped out of her trance when her friends again erupted in noisy laughter.

For the look of the thing, her mouth parted in a smile, but she recognised that where she and Adrian were comparatively sober, one or two of the others were going to be nursing sore heads in the morning. But having missed what had caused such hilarity, before she had a chance to enquire what it was all about, Jolyon, who had somehow manoeuvred it so that he was sitting at her side, suddenly spoke up, not bothering to lower his voice, as he said:

'Don't look now, but somebody over at the next table doesn't like us.'

While the others looked to where Jolyon was looking, Verity had to twist in her seat. Jolyon, she saw, as a blast from the icy grey eyes of a man at the next table met hers head-on, had not been joking!

Arrogantly, she refused to let her eyes be the first to fall away. 'Who would dare to have such nerve?' she said in general to her crowd.

But she was to feel none of the triumph that should have been hers when, favouring her with a glance of contempt, the dark-haired man looked from her, his interest clearly more on the stunning-looking blonde who sat next to him.

Observing that he was with a party of eight and that although champagne seemed to be flowing freely his group did not appear to be having half such a good time as her group were having—they were not making so much noise about it anyway—Verity turned back to her friends to catch the tail end of what Adrian had been saying.

'What did you say?' she asked, all her senses alert as, stone cold sober then, she could swear she had heard the name 'Jepherson'.

'You asked who would have the nerve not to like us,' Adrian obliged. 'I was just saying that I hope the Lower Bassett Country Club can continue in the way it's started out with such topnotch clientele.' And amid laughter so that she had to strain her ears to hear the rest of it, he told her, 'I was saying that beside such top-drawer people as ourselves, they have none other than Holt Jepherson in their midst tonight.'

Miranda and Sadie chose that moment to visit the powder room. But as an ice-cold chill struck at the heart of Verity, hardly believing her hearing, she was forcing a smile to hide the sudden uprush of hate that threatened to consume her, as wanting confirmation, she asked:

'Are you saying that—the man at the table to the left of me—the dark-haired one sitting next to the blonde, is Holt Jepherson?'

'None other.' Adrian fooled by her smile saw none of the hate that sparkled in her eyes. 'Sorry I can't introduce you,' he quipped, 'I only know who he is because I was in my father's office some time back when he came in to enquire about some house or other.'

'Don't fret,' Verity returned, aware, as she froze over, that her smile was slipping. 'They're some people I'd by far prefer not to know.'

CHAPTER TWO

SOMEHOW or other Verity was able to turn the subject away from Holt Jepherson and to keep up a flow of conversation until Miranda and Sadie returned from the powder room. But as soon as they had joined in with the general chatter, Verity backed out to sit with every appearance of interest, but with her thoughts eaten up with the man at the next table.

It was impossible then for her to recapture any of the pleasure to be experienced in an evening out with her friends, and she was to hate Holt Jepherson the more that, not content with ruining what should have been an exciting business career, he should be there to ruin her social life as well.

The meal had finished some thirty minutes ago, and casually, unable to resist another look at the man who was responsible for her dreams turning to ashes, Verity adjusted her seat as though her long legs had been cramped beneath the table. In that position, while still very much a member of her party, the small turn she had given to her chair enabled her to have a good look at the man whom she had so much reason to hate.

The blonde, she saw, was hanging on to his every word—no accounting for taste. But it was not the blonde who interested her.

So that was what a tycoon looked like! He was far younger than she had expected, and looked to be anywhere between thirty and forty. Not that his age concerned her, as with hostile eyes she took in his high intelligent forehead, his average-size nose, and his firm mouth and chin. Oddly then, as she noticed the way he spoke so as not to intrude on the conversation of other diners, was she struck by the sophisticated appearance and behaviour not only of him, but also of the people he was with.

The sharp contrast of the unsophisticated way she and her friends must appear suddenly hit her. But in the next instant she was annoyed that any such realisation should occur to her. And annoyed and angry that just by seeing Holt Jepherson, without even speaking to him—not that she ever would—it should for one moment have her thinking how immature her group must appear. She glared mutinously at him. It was at that moment that he flicked his eyes from the blonde.

What she expected him to do as he caught her eyes full on him, she could not have said. But that he should completely ignore her glaring look, when surely he must have seen it, and, entirely unperturbed, turn his gaze back to his blonde companion, was something Verity had not expected. She was not used to being looked through as though she did not exist, and it rankled. And suddenly there appeared in her an overwhelming urge to do something that would make it impossible for him to ignore her.

'Verity.' Jolyon speaking her name had her slewing round in her seat.

'Jolyon,' she said.

'I was asking if you'd like to dance,' he said, obviously having asked her before, only she hadn't heard.

Verity looked at the dance area where couples, already dancing to a slow smoochy number, were locked in each other's arms.

'I . . .' she began. But, about to refuse—she had no wish to be clasped to Jolyon Robey's chest—she suddenly caught sight of a blonde head preceding a tall, dark-haired man on to the dance floor. 'Why not?' she said. And not stopping to wonder what she had let herself in for, as a smile beamed across Jolyon's face, Verity left her chair and followed in the wake of Holt Jepherson.

Dancing with Jolyon was as bad as she had anticipated. 'Give me room to breathe!' she complained when his arms took her in a grip such as though his life depended upon it.

'Sorry,' he promptly apologised, but he gave her only a couple of more inches breathing space.

Not certain now why she had chased after Holt Jepherson, though it had seemed a good idea at the time, Verity had just started to become completely fed up—Jolyon again holding her too tightly was not making her feel any more cheered—when suddenly she saw that they were dancing right next door to Holt Jepherson and his partner; and while she did not miss the look in the blonde's eyes that were all invitation to the man she was dancing with—no platonic relationship there!—when Jolyon moved in a half turn, suddenly Verity was looking straight into the eyes of the man who had so recently thought her beneath his notice. There was too much hatred and fight in her to let him get away with it a second time!

The band was playing softly when, taking no chance on them playing a sudden crescendo, she raised her voice to tell Jolyon, and everyone close by:

'I'm going home.'

Startled, Jolyon abruptly stopped dancing, which mattered not since with everyone else seeming to have come to crowd the floor, no one was dancing off anywhere in a hurry.

'Home?' he exclaimed. 'But why? I thought you were enjoying yourself?'

'I *was*,' she replied, but finding Holt Jepherson's eyes on her again, she willed him not to look away as, pointing her remarks at no one but him, she added, 'But that was before I became aware of the sort of *riff-raff* the management allows in here.'

As she watched, she saw the cold look that came to the man she was addressing. But he was still not going anywhere, and she hadn't finished yet. And when Jolyon thought to protest, 'I say, that's a bit strong, isn't it?' she had her reply ready.

'Not a bit too strong,' she answered, favouring Jolyon with her shoulder, but not moving further than to face Holt Jepherson full square. 'I know for a fact,' she went on, her eyes glittering with hate, 'that not a million miles from where I'm standing lurks one of the biggest and smoothest usurpers of all time.'

There had been no mistaking the vehemence with which the words left her. But with her eyes fixed on no one but the man she was reviling, she saw that her message had been received by the person it was aimed at. He was not slow on the uptake either, she observed, for his look of puzzlement was soon replaced by a narrowed eyed look of hostility when, for good measure, she tossed in his direction:

'I can feel myself getting contaminated,' and for Jolyon's benefit, 'I'm off.'

Not pausing to wonder why she should suddenly feel all of a tremble inside, Verity wasted no more time. And with Jolyon hard at her heels, begging to know what all that was about, she stuck her nose in the air and headed to their table to pick up her bag.

'I'm off home,' she told the others, declining the chair Rollo had pulled out for her.

'So soon!' exclaimed Miranda.

And while Jolyon forgot his curiosity to get in quickly to ask if she was doing anything tomorrow night, Verity said she would be in touch, and made her farewells. She left the Club just as the band finished playing the last bars of the smoochy number.

She had some way to walk to the car park, but as the cold of the evening hit her, to remind her that it was not unknown for them to have snow in April, so the trembling that had taken her began to wear off.

Half wishing she had stayed to say more, although from memory, Holt Jepherson had received her message that she wasn't about to join his fan club, Verity finally came to her car.

But just when she was about to insert a key into the door lock, her attention was suddenly arrested by the tall, broad-shouldered man who was making his way through the other cars and taking a short cut straight to her.

Adrenalin started to pump as she recognised Holt Jepherson, while at the same time she was recognising that, not liking her remarks, he had come after her. Verity straightened up. And, never one to duck a fight—especially when the right was all on her side—she took a step towards him.

'Didn't you hear enough that you had to come looking for more?' she opened up, to let him know of her awareness that this was no accidental meeting.

Holt Jepherson came to a stop when he reached her, his height this close enabling him to look down on her, for all she had always thought of herself as being tall.

'I didn't hear enough to know what the hell it was you were talking about back there,' he bit, his chin jutting at an aggressive angle.

His aggression did not worry her. She was not afraid of him or any man. Dismissively, she shrugged her shoulders, and bent again to insert her key into the car door lock.

But before metal could make contact with metal, a

hand, as iron-hard as the determination in the man to get to the bottom of what this was all about, had caught hold of her arm and had pulled her round to face him.

On the instant furious that he was daring to add insult to injury by manhandling her, 'Take your tainted hands off me,' Verity flew, outraged, giving her arm a tug.

'I never did care much for innuendo,' gritted Holt Jepherson, that hand on her arm she objected to so much staying precisely where it was. 'Your remarks on that dance floor were directed at me,' he continued, a tough note in his voice that said he was not playing games as, aggressive still, he challenged, 'Haven't you the guts to tell me in private what you hinted at so loudly so that the world and his wife should overhear?'

About to slam into him with a vengeance, to her surprise, Verity found her tongue asking, 'Was that your wife—the blonde?'

'I'm not married,' he clipped.

'Some girl had a lucky escape,' she tossed back. And remembering the way the blonde had looked ready to eat him with her eyes, 'Don't tell me I've ruined a beautiful *friendship* by letting her see that not all women agree that you're the best thing on the menu!'

'It doesn't take too much thinking about to know I'm way down on your list,' he returned sharply, his tone, his look in the floodlit car park area telling her he wasn't likely to lose any sleep over it. 'But I'm still waiting to hear why standing next to me makes you feel contaminated.'

'I suppose it's too much to hope for you to remember every trick you've pulled to get what you want,' Verity flared on an uprush of fresh anger as again she tried to free her arm from his hold, but only to find he was still holding on to her.

'I've tricked you in some way?' he queried, sounding so guilt-free that Verity was sorely tempted to aim a crack at his shin.

'You don't care a damn who you hurt so long as you get your own way, do you?' She was too heated to watch her words as she saw that since her father just *had* to know how much store she had set on being a member of the board, only by trickery could Holt Jepherson have out-manoeuvred him to gain what he was after.

But she was soon to learn that it would be better to watch her tongue where this man was concerned. For as the iron grip on her arm was released, though his tone was still sharp, Holt Jepherson was enquiring:

'You're suggesting I've hurt you in some way?'

Damning her wayward tongue, her pride would never have her owning as much to this sneaky individual. 'Hurt me?' she scoffed, her eyes, her look, everything about her scornful. 'You, Mr Jepherson, just don't have the power to hurt me!'

With that, guessing his lack of surprise that she knew his name must be because he had overheard Adrian telling her who he was, her arm now free, Verity turned again to unlock her car. Though she was to spin round angrily when, coolly, Holt Jepherson did no more than calmly take her car keys from her hand.

'What the hell do you think you're doing?' she exploded, only to have her fury soaring when, as cool as his action, he replied calmly:

'You're in no fit state to drive. I'll get one of your friends to take you h . . .'

'How *dare* you suggest that I'm drunk?' she raged. 'How . . .'

'You've had a few,' he cut in, his voice cool, 'but I'll agree you're far from drunk. Though I think you in turn will have to agree that you're too emotionally overwrought to be in charge of . . .'

'You . . .!' Verity started to screech, and would have borrowed one of Sadie's more choice expressions, had not a particle of dignity come to her aid. Dignity that also said it was beneath her to touch the odious man in any attempt to wrest her car keys from his hands. Drawing herself up tall, she then hissed at him, 'Keep the keys—I don't need them. I can walk!'

She swung from him, ready to make furious tracks out of the car park. But she had gone barely a pace when she felt his hands on her again, his hold firm on her arms as he turned her round to face him.

In an attempt to keep that small amount of dignity, she had just started to count up to ten, though to lay into him physically would give her great satisfaction, when Holt Jepherson broke in through her pugilistic thoughts, to say sharply:

'God knows where you live, but with the nearest house to my knowledge a mile away, you'd freeze with no coat before you came within reach of the first shelter.'

Verity was scornful of him and his obvious knowledge of the small territory Lower Bassett covered. But just as she was determined not to have an ungainly tussle with him for her car keys, she was just as determined that he was not going to humiliate her by going and getting one of her friends to drive her home, and it was airily that she told him:

'I've walked a mile home on a bitterly cold night before.'

But, as she was about to kick his shins if he did not let go of her and let her get on her way, all intention to try for at least a fracture of the bone left her when again she was made to realise that he was just too quick for her. And that, even though there was a touch

of incredulity in his tone, he had soon sifted through
her reply and had come up with:

'You live at Birchwood House!'

His exclamation startled her. Then anger was once
more rushing in that if he knew the name of her home,
then, *behind her back*, he could very well have—been
there!

'You've been to my home!' she exclaimed, appalled.
'My father has *actually* invited you into . . .'

'You're Clement Diamond's daughter!' It was a
toss-up then as to who had received the biggest
shock. But it was he who was the first to recover,
for it was distinctly that Verity heard him mutter,
'My God, I'd heard you were something of a
handful, but . . .' That was as far as she allowed him
to get.

'Who's been talking about me?' she asked hotly, the
prime suspect her Uncle Walter, who had thought her
past redemption ever since, in an outrage of fury when
she was eight, she had charged full pelt at her
fourteen-year-old cousin Basil and shoved him into
the river that ran at the bottom of his home. It had
soon put a stop to him tormenting next door's cat! 'My
father would certainly never . . .' she raged again.
Only this time *she* was chopped off.

'You're shivering,' Holt Jepherson sliced in, when
to her mind she was more shaking with rage than
shivering with cold.

But, as if he had done arguing with her, and despite
her loud voluble protests at such treatment, before she
could begin to wonder what the devil he thought he
was doing, he had forcibly marched her away from her
own car and did not stop until he had taken her to a
sleek limousine parked some way away. And before
she knew it, he had unlocked the vehicle and had
pushed her inside. Whereupon he effectively quashed

any effort she made to rocket from what she guessed was his car, by telling her grimly.

'Either I drive you home or I drag you back in there, and get the soberest member of your party to do the honours.'

'Bombastic swine!' she hissed, frustration and fury mingling. He knew damn well, though *how* he knew, since he didn't know the first thing about her, that she would never lift her head again if he breathed a word to her fun-loving friends that she could be so vulnerable as to be emotionally upset, *she* didn't know.

But before she could start telling him what she thought of his high-handed ways, and to ask who the hell did he think he was that *he* should decide she was not capable of driving not more than a mile up the road, the ignition had been switched on, and the car had moved forward.

'In a hurry all of a sudden,' she sneered, determined to needle him if she could. 'Afraid the blonde won't be so hot for you if you leave her to cool her heels for much longer?'

'For your father's sake, since word has it he dotes on you, I'll see you safely to your door,' he muttered, showing all evidence that he was as gone on Verity Diamond as she was gone on him. 'But you'll forgive me if I don't linger—I have a party I'd prefer to get back to.'

'Celebrating your seat on the board of Diamond Small Tools, no doubt!' she hurled at him, forcing back tears that were suddenly trying to get through. The champagne should have been flowing at her table to celebrate her position on that board, but it had been at his table that the ice buckets had stood.

'Actually, it's a birthday celebration,' Holt Jepherson corrected her, dipping his headlights as the lights of another car came over a rise.

Verity found relief from pressing tears in vitriolic sarcasm, her voice sweetly acid, as she said, 'Do forgive me for not wishing you many happy returns.'

To hear from his short bark of laughter that her unsubtle hope that he never had another birthday had amused him, was the last thing she had expected, or wanted. But, as he thought to tell her that it was not his birthday which was being celebrated, before she could think of anything that would send his sense of humour flying, he had turned the car into the drive of Birchwood House and had pulled to a stop.

She would have bolted from him then, and without thanks. But choked as she was by the confirmation that he must have been to her home before, since, without bothering to ask for directions, he had driven straight there and had slowed down at just the right place for his long car to turn into the concealed drive, she was too taken aback to move. And he, she was to discover, appeared not to be in such a hurry after all, for in full view from the light left on over the porch, he was staying to say:

'I've reasoned by now, of course, that your antipathy must have something to do with my recent connection with Diamond Small Tools.'

'Aren't you the clever one!' she derided.

'But what I haven't been able to fathom,' he went on, only the appearance of the ice chips forming in his eyes telling her that he had heard her, when he ignored her comment, 'is why the deuce you have taken against my joining the board of directors; and why you should charge me with trickery.'

'I don't know how else you could have pulled it off,' Verity snapped, aware she was fast going out of control. 'Only by trickery could you have got my father to go back on his word that that seat would one day be mine. He *promised* me that place on the board,' she cried, 'and *you*—*you* came in and stole it from me!'

She was swallowing hard to keep back tears as she ended. But at the difficulty she was having in suppressing her tears, it was brought home to her that this man had tabbed it correctly when he had said that she was emotionally overwrought.

Needing to get away from him—her tears came out on display for no one—Verity hurriedly left the car, and found the control not to weep while she sorted around in her bag for her door key.

She was not thanking him any more than she had done, when she found he had moved from the car too, and had come to join her on the top doorstep. And while she was still fuming, he said quietly, his voice sounding sincere:

'I didn't know that seat had been promised to you. I ...'

'Would it have made any difference if you had?'

More frustration came to her when, though she wanted that front door key with all speed, the dratted thing was eluding her feverish fingers.

Her fingers had just lighted on the key when, 'No,' he evenly replied, 'it wouldn't.'

'Is it your aim to be on the board of every company in the country?' she asked, not wanting an answer when with trembling fingers she pushed her door key home. But when he did not answer, that did not satisfy her either. And it was angrily that she told him, 'Well, make the most of this one, Mr Jepherson—you won't have this particular seat for very long!'

'You intend to ...' he paused, but his voice was quietly confident when using the word she had used on the dance floor, he ended, '... to usurp—me?'

More than ever wanting to hit him when his quiet confident tone told her he thought she didn't have a chance, she spoke quietly too, as, loathing the very sight of him, she said, 'That seat is mine by right,' and meaning every word, she vowed, 'And I intend to have it!'

He had heard her unshakeable vow, she knew he had. But it was totally unexpected that he should reach out to take hold of her right hand in a formal kind of handshake.

Verity had still not recovered when, looking down at the completely feminine look of her, and sounding just as though he knew something which she did not, the moment before he pushed her in through the front door, he mockingly let fall:

'May the best man win!'

CHAPTER THREE

VERITY awoke early the following morning. But when on other mornings after a late night, she would snuggle down for another hour, that morning, as indignant thoughts of Holt Jepherson sprang into her head, all vestige of sleep went from her.

Not that she had been so very late in coming home last night. There had been other times, she recalled, when it had been the early hours of the morning before she had got home. But, on the instant furious that *that* man had been responsible for her cutting short her evening with her friends, she was to grow even more furious that not only had he marched her to his car to carry out his intent to drive her home but— her own self coming in for some of her fury—she had *let* him!

Unused to being bossed about by anybody, she relived everything that had taken place, and all too soon she was sorely regretting that she had restrained the urge to crack his shins. 'May the best man win,' he had mocked, but in remembering his words, his mockery, she was too angry then to be still. Leaping out of bed, collecting fresh clothes as she went, Verity headed for her adjoining bathroom.

She'd win all right, she fumed, as she stood under the shower. She recalled her feeling that Holt Jepherson knew something she did not, but she also recalled thinking he must have tricked her father to be able to pinch her place in the company. And although no plan of campaign presented itself just then, she re-avowed that—be it by fair means or foul—she would win. She would not rest until Holt Jepherson had been removed from that place that had been promised to her.

Though until that elusive plan of campaign did come to mind, she thought perhaps the time had come for her to make her peace with her father.

But with the recollection, when twenty minutes later she left her room, that because of Holt Jepherson she had a mile to walk to collect her car—though how she was going to get in and drive it if he hadn't left her car keys with the management of the Country Club, she didn't know—Verity's face wore a none too ecstatic expression when she joined her father in the breakfast room.

Clement Diamond lowered his newspaper to take a glance at her as the door opened, and one look was all he needed to know that the war was still on.

'I've told you about it before,' he said grumpily by way of a 'Good morning'.

'What?' she asked, taking her place at the table, and suddenly not liking to be bad friends with him, having a hard time in overcoming her stubbornness since it was he who was in the wrong, not her.

'Leaving your car on the drive all night,' he responded shortly, missing her reaction completely as he pulled his paper in front of him, and complained, 'I don't expect you bothered to lock it, or to take the keys out of the ignition either.'

'I—don't expect I did,' said Verity, getting over her surprise that Holt Jepherson must have driven her car to Birchwood House and got one of his friends to pick him up. Well, that was something else she wasn't going to thank him for either. She wanted no favours from *him*!

In the middle of thinking that if it hadn't been for him she would have driven her car home herself anyway, it occurred to her that maybe she ought to tell her father that she had met him. But with a part of her pushing her to make friends with her father, she just knew she would soon be expressing anger and hostility if she had to say anything about Holt Jepherson; and that would only make things worse, not better, between her and her parent.

Mrs Trueman, coming in at that moment and asking if she was going to have a proper breakfast or just toast, took her mind away from the man who had so outrageously forced her into his car last night.

'Just toast, Trudy, please,' she answered. She was fond of their housekeeper, even if Trudy was sometimes disapproving of her and not averse to telling on her if she thought it was for her salvation.

'You won't get very fat on that,' was Mrs Trueman's opinion as she went out.

Silence stretched after she had gone. But more than ever, as one minute, and then two minutes, ticked by with no sound being heard apart from the rustle of *The Times*, did Verity want things back the way they were with her and her father.

It was as the third minute ticked by that impulse had its head. 'Are you mad at me because I went to the new Country Club?' she asked in a rush.

'You're over twenty-one,' her parent replied stiffly, to let her know that while she thought she had reached her majority three years ago, in his book the majority age was still twenty-one.

The ice broken, it took Verity a deal of effort to push behind her all memory of how bitterly disappointing attaining the age of twenty-one had turned out to be.

'It's—not much of a club,' she said after a second or two. And because he was her father, and she did love him, 'I don't think I shall go there again,' she conceded.

To see him put down his paper, and to observe, although he maintained a straight face, that there was something of a twinkle in his eyes as he stood up ready to leave for his office, and to hear that note of teasing in his voice as going to the door, he murmured, 'Surely to God they haven't barred you already!' brought a grin to Verity's mouth.

Her heart lighter than it had been since she had started hostilities with him, when Trudy came in to clear away Verity, impulsive still, volunteered:

'I'll clear the table if you like.'

'You're up to something,' said the canny house-keeper suspiciously, having lived through the fire and tempest of her young mistress's growing years, and being the least likely to have the wool pulled over her eyes.

'No, I'm not!' denied Verity, and was quite as innocent as she looked—until she thought about it. 'Well,' she qualified, her thoughts on how wouldn't she be up to something—and with a vengeance—once that elusive plan to oust Holt Jepherson materialised, 'I could be,' she owned, her streak of basic honesty showing through. 'But it's nothing you need tell my father about.' And, her grin coming out, 'He'll be pleased with the end result, I promise you.'

'I'm pleased to hear it,' said Trudy. Dipping her hand into her overall pocket, she fished out Verity's car keys and placed them on the table, and unable to hold back a smile, 'I don't tell your father *everything* you get up to,' she said.

'Where did I drop them?' Verity thought to ask, her look of innocence not so natural this time.

'In the letter box,' Trudy replied, and went out with an air of someone unsurprised at anything Verity did.

After wheeling the used crockery into the kitchen, Verity spent the next few hours searching every avenue for some scheme which would put the skids under Holt Jepherson. She had an imaginative mind, and consequently some of her ideas went far beyond the realms of possibility. Though she had to admit that she did rather enjoy the picture that came to mind of every other member of the board ganging up on their latest recruit. The vision in her mind's eye of seeing him standing tarred and feathered was little short of beautiful.

But, try as she might, no idea came that was feasible enough to work through from beginning to end, and which would ultimately see her father kicking him off the board.

Needing a break from such constant fruitless thinking, Verity decided to ring Miranda for a chat. But she wished she had allowed some space in her thoughts to realise that her car had most likely still been in the car park of the Country Club when Miranda had left, for she was quickly having to come up with some excuse when Miranda told her that Jolyon, seeing her car, had wanted to get up a search party to look for her.

'I decided to walk home,' Verity told her, not liking to lie to her friend but pride demanding that no one should know that she hadn't had any choice but to submit to that authoritarian brute's refusal to allow her to drive.

'Were you over the limit?' asked Miranda, accepting that since she had a fear of being caught flouting the drinking and driving law of the land, Verity had thought better than to risk getting stopped by the police.

'I'm never sure what the legal limit is,' Verity evaded, certain she had been well inside it. And turning the conversation, 'What time did you leave the Club?'

'Not long after you. Jolyon was fed up after you left, and you know Jolyon when he's fed up – he's a proper drag. Anyway, we headed him off calling out a search party, and went back to Sadie's place, where Rollo put her through the third degree about living on her own.'

'Do you think he wants to live on his own?' Verity asked.

'I think he's torn between not wanting to be answerable to his father, while at the same time wanting all the comforts of home,' said Miranda, and leaving the conversation there, 'Fancy doing anything special tonight?'

'I think I'll have a night in,' replied Verity, and found she was again being evasive when Miranda said:

'I haven't liked to ask what happened when you stayed home the other evening,' but having respected Verity's silence on the subject for so long, she couldn't resist, 'Did your father . . .'

'I'll tell you about it some time,' interrupted Verity quickly. And she was glad that Miranda was friend enough to leave it there, as the other girl went on to suggest:

'Do you feel like a trip up to town tomorrow?'

'Why not?' she agreed. London was within easy commuting distance of Lower Bassett, given that she'd have to drive into the nearest town and leave her car in the station yard, and she hadn't been to London in ages.

Deciding that they would take an early train, they chatted for a few minutes more, then said goodbye, Miranda to go to a hairdressing appointment, Verity to go back to trying to find some way of giving Holt Jepherson his come-uppance.

But within minutes she was again lifting up the

telephone receiver, this time in order to take a call. Though had she known who her caller was, it was certain that the phone would have rung for ever before she would have lifted a finger to answer it.

As it was, to hear the cultured tones of Holt Jepherson announcing himself so amazed her that what should have been her first instinct—to slam the phone down again, hard—escaped her. And he had asked how was she that morning before she had got herself fully together.

'I don't have a hangover,' she said smartly into the mouthpiece. And, attempting to give him something to blunt his ego on, 'I wasn't drunk *before* I had the sobering experience of having to talk to you!'

His ego had surfaced without a bruise, she heard when, his tones even, he enquired, 'Then I'm to believe that, sober, you meant all you said? That this morning you still think me the usurper who has to be—er—unseated?'

At his mockery, her mercury soared, 'Don't make yourself too comfortable,' she snapped. 'You won't be there that long!' She did then what she should have done in the first place—down went the phone.

Rat-fink, swine! she fumed, minutes passing before she could think to stop pacing the floor and throw herself into an easy chair. He'd obviously phoned to speak to her father, but he hadn't been able to resist having his little gloat when it had been she who had answered the phone, had he? The thought touched briefly that Holt Jepherson must think her father only a part-time chairman if he had expected him to be home at this time of the day, but it had no chance to linger. Oh, why was that plan to get rid of him so elusive?

By the time she joined her father for dinner that night, Verity's temper had cooled. She had spent an abortive afternoon in her search for some way in which to eject Holt Jepherson from her rightful place, but in the end she had realised that the reason why no design was forthcoming must be that she just did not know enough about him.

Dinner was almost over when she decided to rectify that omission. Though she had to lower her eyes so her father should not see the sparkle of hate for the man whose very name she loathed, as she enquired:

'Does—Holt Jepherson live around here?'

On her best behaviour all evening, she was aware of her parent's sudden speculative look. But she kept her mouth smiling and hoped he was remembering that it was she who had offered the olive branch that morning and, genuine as that olive branch had been, that he would conclude that she was leaning over backwards to accept something which, in truth, she would die sooner than accept.

He cleared his throat, and she guessed he was wondering if the armistice was to be a short one. But, as if he had decided to accept her question at face value, at long last he gave her the benefit of the doubt and replied:

'He recently moved into a house over at Drake's Knighton.'

Verity recalled she had once driven through Drake's Knighton, which by her reckoning was some thirty or forty miles away, and as equidistant as Lower Bassett to London. But in her view, thirty or forty miles away was not far enough.

'Where did he live before?' Guilelessly she selected an orange from the fruit bowl and began to peel it.

'In London,' said Clement Diamond after another speculative look at her. 'He still has a flat there, I believe.'

'I expect he wanted his wife and children to have

the benefit of some country air,' smiled Verity, wondering how she could deceive her father so when always before, no matter if she knew she was going to be 'for it', she had never hidden behind deceit. But she quieted her conscience that needs must when, in this case, she was driving that devil—out.

'Holt isn't married,' she was informed.

Her temper came perilously near to fraying to hear her father call that outsider by his first name—just as though they were big buddy-buddies! But she concealed her flare of anger by feigning to be just the teeniest bit bored with the subject, to venture, 'I expect he's bald, fat and ninety,' which brought a smile to Clement Diamond's face.

'I'll introduce you some time,' he suggested idly, but Verity did not miss the probing in his casual suggestion that told her he was searching for confirmation that she was over her terrible disappointment.

From somewhere she summoned up a smile, and having heard not nearly enough yet about that arrogant mocking swine, she took a leaf from her father's casually probing book, and pressed to know more.

But when she went to bed that night, anxious as she had been not to betray anything of what lay behind her questions because, although he gave her a lot of rope her father was no fool where she was concerned, she found she had gleaned very little.

Sleep miles away, she lay in her bed and mused that she had already known that Holt Jepherson was unmarried. And she couldn't see that knowing he lived at Drake's Knighton was going to be instrumental in getting her what she wanted. And she just hadn't needed her father to repeat again, as he had, how highly thought of Holt Jepherson was in the business world, and how he personally found him to be a man who could be totally relied upon in business.

Verity warmed to Miranda that at no time as they chatted as they did the round of their favourite London stores the next day, did she press to hear what had taken place between her and her father on that never-to-be-forgotten night. Verity still was not ready to share her hurt with anyone.

On the return train journey, it was arranged that she would drive over to Miranda's house that night, and that they would take it from there to decide how they would spend that Saturday evening.

'See you some time after eight,' Miranda reaffirmed when Verity had helped to carry her packages to her car. 'I should have some energy back by then.'

As she pulled out of the station car park the smile that had been in Verity's face at her friend's remark faded. Into her head popped thoughts of the man she had been pushing into the background all day.

She let herself into Birchwood House, her face set as she recalled that Holt Jepherson had suspected her hurt. Even though she had hotly denied his, 'You're suggesting I've hurt you,' it told her that she had given him some hint of her vulnerability.

Damning him, and everything about him, as she went along the hall, so deeply involved with her thoughts was she that she wasn't quick enough to change her expression when Mrs Trueman appeared from the other direction.

'You're not going to feel any more happy when I tell you that Jolyon Robey has phoned three times today,' Trudy greeted her.

'You wouldn't like to tell him I've got a date tonight if he rings again, would you?'

'Do your own dirty work,' sniffed Trudy, but her mouth had a goodhumoured look to it.

'I will,' said Verity. But she was not thinking of Jolyon Robey as she said it.

With her father spending the evening dining and playing his beloved Bridge with some friends, Verity, having previously advised Trudy that she would have a meal at midday in London, went up to her room to shower and to change into something that would be suitable for whatever she and Miranda elected to do.

'Can I get you something to eat?' the food-orientated Trudy asked when Verity sought her out in the kitchen some short while later.

'I'll get it. I only want something light. How about you?' Verity thought to ask. 'Fancy some of my famous scrambled egg?'

Trudy was of the opinion that Verity's whiter-than-white jump-suit would come to grief if she went anywhere near the stove, and they were wrangling amicably on who was going to be chef, when suddenly the front doorbell pealed.

'That settles it,' said Trudy with the ease of being a long established part of the family. 'You be doorman—I'll be cook.'

'You're getting bossy in your old age,' said Verity, accepting defeat with a smile.

But that word bossy had brought Holt Jepherson to mind, and as she went along the hall, her smile disappeared. Fleetingly, she realised that since that man seemed to be almost constantly in her mind anyway, it was no wonder that any word, look, or happening should bring a reminder of him.

With a determined effort she pushed him from her head. And although she was unable to summon up another smile, she was of the view, as she reached the front door, that if Jolyon Robey had called round with the hope of tagging along when she went to Miranda's, she was just going to be more blunt with him than to date she had been.

Though to see when she pulled back the door that it was not Jolyon Robey standing there, but none other than Holt Jepherson, was to render her speechless. But while she was regaining the power of her vocal cords, while, oddly, at the same time she acknowledged that where he had looked quite something in his dinner jacket the other night, nothing seemed to be detracted from him when he was now wearing a dark sweater and slacks, Holt Jepherson was taking the initiative by stepping over the threshold, murmuring smoothly:

'I've caught you in, I see.'

Not disposed to give him top marks for his vision, Verity only just managed to keep her temper at his cool cheek in inviting himself in by knowing that it must be her father he had called to see.

'I'm going out shortly,' she told him coldly. But she could not help the faint tinge of a purr when she sweetly told him, 'My father must have forgotten you were going to call. He went out for the evening ages ago.'

Any hope she might have had to deflate him that her father considered his appointment with him so insignificant, that he had forgotten all about it, fell to the ground like a lead balloon.

'He's playing Bridge at the Garnhams',' Holt Jepherson told her equably, clearly having known before he'd rung the bell that he would not find Clement Diamond at home. And, his temper staying equable, he went on to rebuke, 'Had you stayed to listen when I rang yesterday, instead of losing that wayward temper of yours, you could have saved me this visit.'

Startled that yesterday's call had not been for her father, and that it was not to see her father that he was here now, Verity ignored his remark about her wayward temper, and not liking it at all that the enemy should come into her camp, she was quickly exclaiming:

'You've come to see me!'

He turned to attend to the closing of the front door, in no hurry to get started, apparently, although she had told him she would shortly be going out. But by the time he was again facing her Verity, with no intention of inviting him further into her home, had got her second wind.

'May I ask to what I owe this dubious pleasure?' she queried sarcastically, not missing the sudden glint that came to his eyes, for all it was quickly masked. 'Oh, I get it,' she drawled, never intending to back down where he was concerned, glint or no glint, 'You've come to beg me not to push you out of that place you filched.'

She did have to award him some marks, she conceded, that when she knew full well he had not taken kindly to her sarcasm, he managed still to retain his even tone when, accepting that anything he had to say would be said in the hall, he told her:

'I phoned yesterday, primarily to hope to repair any damage that ensued from us getting off on the wrong foot.'

Heavens! she thought. Surely he wasn't suggesting that he and she be friends! 'And there was I thinking you rang just so you could have a go at me about my drinking habits,' she jibed, allowing sarcasm a free rein.

She caught sight of that glint again. That glint this time accompanied by a movement in his jaw that told her he was hanging on grimly to his self-control. She was not surprised to hear him take a deep and steadying breath, before he replied:

'You've had one hell of a disappointment, Verity Diamond. And for that I'll excuse the fact that your manners leave a lot to be desired.'

He'd excuse her! Her temper given a boost, she was just about to slam into him, when, before she could start, he quietly cut the ground from under her, by saying, 'I've called here tonight, not for you, and not for me, but for your father's sake.'

'My father!' she exclaimed, her temper gone in a flash at the intimation that there was something amiss with her father. 'What do you mean?' she asked quickly. And, not giving herself time to think that if there was something ailing her father then she would be the one more likely to know about it than Holt Jepherson, 'What's wrong with him?' she panicked; her panic observed, as he replied:

'Nothing—so far as I know. But he works damned hard holding that firm together.'

Relief surging in, acid came to the surface as she recovered from fear that her father might have a heart condition or something of the sort which he had kept from her.

'There was nothing wrong with the firm before you joined it,' she told him, his sharp-eyed look not lost on her. Though, apparently, her vitriol was lost on him. For he had walked straight over what she had just said, when he replied:

'Your father works harder than many men half his age.' And going pertinaciously on to explain why he had called, 'That being so, it occurred to me—since in your eyes I appear to be the villain of the piece—that in the interests of him having rest and a harmonious home life, I should make the first approach to try and reach some sort of understanding.'

All that Verity understood—she had no intention of telling him she had already made her peace with her

father, even if she would never rest until that promise
he had made her had been kept—was that this man
had what was rightfully hers, and that she wanted it
back!

'You're suggesting that I give my father hell when
he gets home?'

'At a guess,' he replied, 'if you're serving him any of
the same sort of flak you serve me,' a quirk appeared
unexpectedly at the corners of his mouth to tell her
just how much any of the flak she directed his way
affected him, 'then I'd say he's having a pretty hard
time one way and another.'

Aware that she had not been the sweetest person in
the world to live with in those recent days after her
father had burst the bubble of her rosy dreams, it was
huffily that she asked, 'Why should that concern you?'

'I respect and admire Clement for all he's achieved,'
he answered shortly, giving her an exasperated look that
she couldn't or wouldn't see what he was getting at.

'So?' she asked, feeling herself growing prickly
again because Holt Jepherson should take it upon
himself to tell her how much her father had achieved,
when no one could be more aware than she was how,
in those early days of Diamond Small Tools, he had
worked long into the night to make the company the
valuable, not to say superior, firm it was today.

'So,' he said tautly, his aggression coming out to
meet hers, 'he's earned his rest when he arrives home.'

'How philanthropic!' she scorned. But the heat in
her was to dip as she remembered the look of strain
that had been on her father not so long back. Though
recalling that all signs of strain had gone from him
recently, she felt indignant when, careless that Holt
Jepherson seemed to be looking for an outlet for his
aggression, she charged, 'Or is it, I wonder, just that
you'd like my father to rest at home—permanently?'

'What the devil is that supposed to mean?' he charged straight back, his aggression breaking.

'Just this,' she snapped, her eyes starting to flash fire. 'Having snaffled my place, your only interest in my father resting is so that you can nudge him over and snaffle the chairman's seat as well!'

'You . . .' For a moment, in that second before he had grabbed back his hold on his temper, Verity thought the least she would receive would be a name similar to the one she had nearly borrowed from Sadie that night in the car park. But, although his control on his temper was thin, and he looked in no way less angry, whatever he had been going to say was amended to a muttered, 'My stars, Walter Diamond wasn't joking when he said you were a handful!' But before she could make any reply to that, he was to send her blood soaring to boiling point when he told her toughly, 'You might be twenty-one, Verity Diamond, but it's about time you bloody well grew up and learned to accept, and to swallow, life's disappoint . . .'

'Don't you *dare* tell me to grow up!' she erupted, sparks flashing from her eyes as, enraged by his tough remarks, she flew on: 'If I'd been born a boy like my Uncle Walter's precious Basil, you wouldn't have had the chance to cheat me out of my birthright!'

Furiously she had roared to an end, but to her utter astonishment, suddenly she saw that every scrap of aggression had left Holt Jepherson. And as his eyes slowly drifted over her definitely feminine shape, he had effectively nullified her fury, when, his voice now as even as it had been when he had first arrived, warmth taking the ice out of the appreciative grey eyes, he said:

'What a loss to the world that would have been.'

'W-What?' she stuttered, swinging from being ready

and waiting for a pitched battle, into a sudden state of confusion at his change of tack.

'Angry or composed,' he advised, 'your face is beautiful. Your figure matches it. To have been born a boy would . . .'

'Cut out the soft soap, Jepherson,' Verity chopped him off before he could go further. But, uncaring that he thought her beautiful, she was sufficiently sidetracked to leave the core of their argument, and to remember the blonde in his party that particular night. 'Mine isn't the first beautiful face you've clapped eyes on,' she said sourly.

'You're thinking of Selene Aston?' he queried, when she didn't want him reading her thoughts. And he succeeded in niggling her the more, when she wasn't used to being ignored, when he went momentarily from her to murmur, 'A delightful creature.'

'And one who wouldn't dream of going against *any* of your wishes,' she retorted tartly.

His brow coming down told her he didn't think too much of her comment, even before he rapped, 'If that remark was meant to imply that Selene is my mistress, then I thought better of you.'

'That she's your mistress goes without saying,' Verity rapped right back, not of a mind to be put down by him or anyone else. 'But for your information, I have better things to do than to give a thought to whom you do or do not sleep with.' And having put him straight about that, 'The only implication was that from what I could see, the lovely blonde looked to be so besotted that she would willingly move over to let you have her seat on any board her father happened to be chairman of.'

When at the end of her self-vindication, Holt Jepherson, his brow clearing, just stood and looked at her, Verity had the terrible feeling that she had again inadvertently let him see just how much her father's broken promise hurt her. But, although she was ready for him if he made the smallest crack about it, the only reply he made was a mocking:

'Wouldn't your friend do the same for you?'

'You mean—Jolyon Robey?' she asked.

'If he was the one you were dancing with,' he agreed. And when she neither needed nor wanted his opinion, 'Not your style, I would have thought.'

'What do you mean by that?' she flared aggressively. Even while she might agree with him that Jolyon was not her type, nobody cast aspersions on her friends and got away with it.

'Put your hackles down,' he replied evenly. 'I wasn't suggesting any fault in Robey's character, merely stating that from what I know of you, I'd say you need to marry a man who can . . .'

'Marry!' she exclaimed, the answer that she had no intention of marrying Jolyon Robey there in her exclamation. Though, suddenly aware that her exclamation might have sounded derisory to Jolyon who, whatever he was, was still a friend, she did the best she could to turn it, by adopting a sophisticated pose, and drawling, 'Does anyone marry these days?'

'A good few, I believe.'

'But not you?' she enquired. And with saccharine sweetness, she found small delight in the dig, 'I'd say you're fast running out of time, Mr Jepherson, if you're waiting for "little Miss Right" to come along.'

Her dig had not touched him. Nor did it please her at all to see from his sudden grin that he had again been amused by something she had said.

'At thirty-six I think I've still a few years ahead before I can be called a confirmed bachelor,' he commented.

To her surprise, when she just knew that she was

not at all interested in his love life, her tongue was again behaving independently of her, as it brought her to ask, 'You're thinking of marrying Selene Aston?'

'Would you have any objection?'

Sarcasm she just didn't need. It was at that point that Verity decided that she had already given Holt Jepherson too much of her time. 'I've only one objection,' she tossed at him as she crossed to the door and pulled it wide, 'and you don't need me to repeat what that is.'

'Figured out a way to unseat me yet?' he enquired, undisturbed, as he joined her at the door and denied her full the pleasure of throwing him out, by flicking a glance at his watch as if to suggest that he too was running late for his evening appointment and must be on his way.

'I'm working on it,' she told him waspishly.

'Don't overstrain the grey matter, Miss Diamond,' he murmured in passing. But heartily did she wish that his evening appointment was not so suddenly urgent. For as his farewell floated back, he was gone before she could punch his head for the, 'You haven't a prayer,' that reached her.

Slamming the door hard shut after him, Verity was incensed at the challenge she saw in his words. It was as if he was just *daring* her to do her worst! She—Verity Diamond—who, any one of her friends could tell him, had never backed away from a dare in her life!

CHAPTER FOUR

VERITY went down to breakfast the following Friday, feeling no more settled than she had felt all that week. Not only was she frustrated, but she was utterly fed up that, no matter how hard or for how long she had thought, still nothing had occurred to her—short of murder—as a way to take up the insufferable Holt Jepherson's challenge.

'Morning, Dad,' she greeted her father when she entered the breakfast room, her voice as flat as she herself was feeling.

Her greeting replied to, she had taken her place at the table and had reached for the coffee-pot, before she became aware that instead of returning to his paper, *The Times* was still lowered, and that her father, his look keen, was observing her over the rim of his spectacles.

'Are you feeling all right?' he asked at her enquiring glance.

'Fine,' she answered, injecting a brightness she did not feel into her reply—her war was no longer with her father, but was with Holt Jepherson—it was a private war.

'You stayed in last night,' Clement Diamond recalled. '*And* the night before, if memory serves,' he added, as if he could not believe she was as 'fine' as she was making out if she had stayed home for two nights on the trot.

Verity dredged up a teasing grin to enquire, 'What's so remarkable about that?' She was fond of all her friends, and she found that even to him she could not voice the disloyalty she had felt when they had all been together on Tuesday, that, save for Miranda, and possibly Adrian, the others had suddenly seemed to be dreadfully callow.

He forbore to answer, but, when never before had she known him to not have an avid interest in the items his paper held, when his paper stayed down and, to her surprise, she saw he was looking a shade uncomfortable, all her instincts were alerted. He had something to say, she was sure of it. And although she had no clue to what that something was, she felt certain that it was something which she was not going to like.

'It's—too much to hope, I suppose,' he said after another few seconds of mulling it over, his voice too casual to fool her for a minute, 'that you'll be in tonight?'

She had no plans for that evening either. But instead of coming straight out and saying so, put off by his cagey—for all he was trying to hide it—attitude, she played cagey too.

'Are we having something special for dinner?' she enquired smilingly, only to be shattered when he came down off the fence and told her:

'We're having—a special guest to dinner.'

By Harry, she thought, were her instincts right to think she was not going to like what she was to hear! She knew all his friends, and most of his business colleagues. It didn't take too much intelligence for her to know that since at some time or other most of them had dined at Birchwood House, the 'special guest' must be a newcomer! But, appalled that her father could be so insensitive to not only invite to dinner the man on whose account his promise to her had been broken, but that he should expect her to be there to play hostess, only by reminding herself that her war with Holt Jepherson was a private war did she manage to stay outwardly calm.

'Oh, what a pity!' she exclaimed, hardly able to credit her acting ability. 'The reason I've had two early nights in a row is that I've got a heavy party tonight.' She even managed to look regretful as she went on, 'Will your guest be offended that I won't be here for dinner?' And knowing damn well who their 'special guest' was to be, 'Who is it—anyone I know?' she enquired.

'You—haven't met him,' said Clement Diamond slowly. 'But after the other evening when you showed such interest in him, and didn't, as I thought you might, become upset when I suggested I would introduce you to him, I thought you might . . .'

'Holt Jepherson?'

He nodded, and looked relieved that she had accepted quite without fuss who his guest was to be. Although, 'Do you mind?' he thought to ask.

Just how much she minded, he would never know. Though realising that since an invitation to dine had been extended and accepted it must mean that the two had recently been in contact, and that Holt Jepherson could not have said anything to her parent about them previously having met, at the same time Verity was fending off having to lie to her father's direct question of 'Do you mind?'

'Did you invite him especially so we could be introduced?' she asked.

'Hm—for the most part,' he replied, but he was beginning to look uncomfortable again as he added, 'Though we do have a great deal of business to discuss. He's—staying the night, actually.'

'Staying the night!' Her voice had risen before she could control it. But quickly she covered her anger that as if it wasn't bad enough that Holt Jepherson was going to have his feet under their dining room table, he was going to sleep under the roof of Birchwood House as well! She forced a smile as she excused her startled exclamation by saying, 'I thought you said he lived quite near?'

'Drake's Knighton is only an hour or so's run away, I'll agree,' said Clement Diamond, looking relieved that she was not objecting but that she had merely been surprised that with Drake's Knighton not so far away, he had invited his associate to stay overnight. 'But with so much business to discuss, it could well be gone midnight before we're through.'

Verity got the picture. Though she was sure she was not bothered that for all her father had tried to make out that Holt Jepherson had been invited into their home so that they should be introduced, he had been invited more because he and her father had matters to talk about. Matters, apparently, which could be better gone over away from a business environment, even if it did look as though they were going to have a late-night sitting.

When Clement Diamond left for his office, she no longer had any need to hide the fact that she was feeling far from happy. She was still in the breakfast room, deep in glum thought, when Mrs Trueman came in to clear away.

'As bad as all that, is it?' the housekeeper questioned after one look at her face.

Verity found a small smile for her, and while the housekeeper got busy clearing the table, she deliberated whether to tell her to prepare for their overnight guest. The idea of leaving Holt Jepherson to make his own bed was almost too sweet to be denied. But in the end, for her father, who prided himself on his hospitality, she found her voice to state:

'We're having company tonight.'

'I know,' replied Trudy, to shake her. 'Your father asked me last night to get the best guest room ready, and to . . .'

'He asked you last night!' Only then, as her exclamation gave away that she had only just heard about it, did it dawn on Verity that her father must have known before this morning that they were to have company, but that, when she had been in for all last evening, he must have been so unsure of her reaction that he had left it until now to tell her!

'He probably forgot all about it after that,' said Trudy, to smooth things over, when she knew as well as Verity that Clement Diamond had the memory of an elephant.

'I must have triggered off his memory when I said I wouldn't be in to dinner tonight,' said Verity, joining in the face-saving game.

'Given in to Jolyon Robey's pestering?' teased Trudy.

'Which reminds me,' said Verity, leaving her chair, 'I've got a few phone calls to make.'

A few telephone calls later, with various ideas for an evening's entertainment being considered and then rejected, the outcome was that Sadie Knowles would have a party if they all brought their own food.

With Trudy busy preparing the best guest room, Verity spent most of the morning in conjuring up a spinach quiche and a cheese and onion quiche to take to the party, her efforts turning out surprisingly well in view of her mutinous thoughts about their 'special guest'.

Her father too came in for some of her mutiny as she recalled the many times in the past that he had complained about her friends. But he'd had no objection to make about her going to a heavy party tonight, had he? He wouldn't want her there tonight when the business discussions, in which she had no part, got under way, would he?

It was mid-afternoon, as she dwelt on her father's reluctance to tell her of his house guest, that her mood changed, and her mutiny softened. And it was love for her parent that brought her round to the view that instead of refusing to shake hands with Holt Jepherson, for the sake of her father's monumental pride, he should find that any fears he might nurse that she might make a scene were completely groundless.

Her plans to be so charming to Holt Jepherson, so that her father would applaud how well she had taken the bitter pill he had served her, took a sharp downward dive when from her bedroom window she saw Holt Jepherson arrive.

By the time she had pulled her resolve back up off the floor and had gone down the stairs to act the perfect hostess, Verity found him in the drawing room standing with her father passing the few conversational minutes of his arrival.

'I'm so sorry I wasn't down to meet you,' she greeted him, her tones warm but not over-effusive as she went forward with her hand outstretched.

'My—er—daughter, Verity,' Clement Diamond said unnecessarily after a moment or two of looking at her a trifle suspiciously. 'Verity, this is Holt Jepherson, who has recently . . .'

Swiped my seat on the board, she almost finished for him, when clearly the words had stuck in his throat. Well, she'd be damned if she would go as far as to congratulate him! 'My father tells me you've recently moved into a house at Drake's Knighton,' she murmured, wanting her hand back from the firm clasp Holt Jepherson, without saying a word, had taken it in.

'Do you know Drake's Knighton?' he enquired, as hellbent, apparently, if one didn't look into his eyes and see the amused gleam there, as she was on playing this game of polite manners to perfection.

'I've passed through it,' she replied as he let go her hand, but those amused grey eyes making her think that, in front of her father, she might yet be giving Holt Jepherson something unamusing to think about. 'I noticed your overnight grip is still in the hall,' she said, and looking at her father, 'Shall I show Mr Jepherson his room?'

Her father's smile, she thought, must be the only natural one in the room. For any suspicion that this was the lull before the storm had gone from his eyes, she saw, when he smiled at how well things were going.

'Would you like to, Verity?' he agreed.

Hoping it wasn't showing that she would sooner show Holt Jepherson the front door than the best guest room, she smiled in his direction before she suggested that he might wish to follow her.

Out in the hall Verity waited a moment while the lounge-suited Holt Jepherson retrieved his hand-grip. Then side by side they ascended the wide staircase. But when, her father no longer there, she had not one word which she wanted to say to their guest, Holt Jepherson, with a sideways glance to her set expression, remarked, 'May I say how delightful you look, Verity, in that creation you're wearing,' and she thought she ought to put him straight if he thought she had donned the flame-coloured dress for his benefit.

'I won't see you at dinner,' she advised him coldly, opening the door of the guest room and pushing it wide. 'I . . .'

'You're not telling me I'm being abandoned for Robey!' he exclaimed in mock horror, to demonstrate just how much the lack of her presence at dinner would affect his appetite.

'I'll show you my engagement ring when I get home,' she snapped, telling herself she was darn sure she wasn't worried at the lack of difference it made to him whether she ate at home that night or where she fed herself, of if she fed herself at all.

Though as all amusement left his expression and, his tone abrupt, he asked, 'You're getting engaged?' she recovered from the oddest sensation of a moment before that, had she not known better, she might have labelled a sense of rejection.

'I think you'll find you have all you need,' she said, ignoring his question. 'But if you need anything, don't hesitate to ask Mrs Trueman—our housekeeper.'

With that, she left him. She was fully aware that she would have told any other guest to contact her should they require anything they were short of. But if he had not got the general idea yet that she would rather do him a disservice than the other way around, perhaps her parting remark might go some way towards enlightening him.

Going along to her room, she idled there for some minutes, musing that while she felt no interest in going to the party she had instigated, it was much too early to drive around to Sadie's when things would not begin to warm up until gone nine.

But when it came back to her that she had experienced the most peculiar feeling when Holt Jepherson had let her know just how much he would not be crying in his soup that she wouldn't be there at the dinner table, Verity became fed up with her own company.

'Having something nice for dinner?' she asked Trudy when she went downstairs to the kitchen to pick up the things she had made for Sadie's party.

'And how!' said Trudy expressively. 'Aren't you sorry you're going out?'

'Not a bit,' said Verity emphatically, but with time to kill, 'Can I make you a cup of tea?'

'I always knew there was good in you,' was the dry reply.

Though as Verity, keeping from under the housekeeper's busy feet, made a pot of tea, involuntarily she found herself asking, 'Have I been such a pain, Trudy?'

'Where would you like me to start?' was the teasing answer, which was no answer, and caused the housekeeper to remark, after a glance at her young mistress's serious expression, 'You'll settle down when Mr Right appears.'

Which remark had Verity's thoughts going straight to Holt Jepherson. But only because, she realised, of the remark she had made to him about him running out of time if he was waiting for 'little Miss Right' to come along.

While she was waiting for the tea to brew, she took the two plates of quiche to her car. She then returned to the kitchen and whiled away another half hour, until she could see that Trudy would prefer to be by herself to concentrate on the repast she was making to delight the palate of the 'special guest'.

Verity said, 'Cheerio,' to her, and went to the drawing room where she thought her father might be, to tell him she was off. He *was* in the drawing room, but so too was Holt Jepherson.

'I'm on my way,' she said, noticing, although she wasn't looking at him, that he had risen from his chair. 'I'll see you when I see you,' she told her father, it being borne in on her that in his presence she was going to have to make some polite utterance to his guest too.

'Have a good time,' her parent instructed, and she was grateful to him that in front of the other man he did not add, as he sometimes did, his part comic, 'And for the lord's sake don't do anything I shall have to come and bail you out for!'.

She turned from him, the smile gone from her eyes but still there on her mouth, as she offered a well brought up, 'Goodnight, Mr Jepherson. I'll . . .'

'Holt, please,' he interrupted smoothly, his height, his sophistication, everything about him seeming suddenly to dominate, so that try as she might—she just could not look away from him.

But, never having been affected by nerves before, to feel strangely shaky inside made Verity determine she was not going to be affected by nerves now. She blinked, and broke that unseen magnetic thread that had so unbelievably kept her eyes fixed to his.

'Goodnight—Holt,' she said politely, after a struggle only she knew about. 'Perhaps I shall see you at breakfast.'

Sadie's party followed the same usual pattern. But where always before Verity had found some degree of enjoyment at such functions, it had only just struck eleven when she was beginning to wonder how much longer she could stick it out.

Jolyon, spotting that she was not dancing, was by her side in a flash. 'I've brought you a drink,' he said, pushing a glass so eagerly into her hand that some of it splashed down her dress and had him apologising profusely as he dabbed at her skirt with his handkerchief, to succeed in knocking her arm and to make more spill over.

Oh grief, she inwardly groaned, and wished she was home and in her bed, Jolyon's gauche antics contrasting overwhelmingly with the sophistication of Holt Jepherson.

She didn't want to think about Holt Jepherson, but he was there in her mind, and wouldn't leave. He was still there in her head, the reason for her not wanting to go home until she could be sure he had retired for the night, while Jolyon regaled her with some tale she might have thought funny a fortnight ago, but which in the frame of mind she found herself, was boring her out of her skull.

But, as luck would have it, Sadie had invited a few other girl friends, and one of them had taken a shine to Jolyon. And he had only just come to the end of his tale, though he was about to start on another equally boring epic, when a new voice said, 'Can I borrow your man for a moment?'

'Treat him gently,' laughed Verity in her relief, as the flattered Jolyon was pulled away to dance.

But inside seconds Verity was back to not feeling at all like laughing. And when she heard someone say that the ice cubes were running low, she was glad to volunteer to fetch more, and to escape to the kitchen.

It was there that she tried to get her spirits up. Always in the thick of whatever was going on, she did not want any of the others to know how depressed she felt.

But, needing her moment or two of solitude, she had just put her hand to the freezer door, when Miranda swung into the kitchen. And it soon became plain that, knowing her better than most, Miranda had not missed that she was not her usual self.

'Having a good time,' Verity got in first.

'You're not,' stated Miranda. And, ready to help if she could, 'I've seen you dancing and laughing like the rest of us, but your heart isn't in it, is it?'

Aware that her friend knew her too well to be deceived, Verity did her the courtesy of not lying to her. 'I'm—a bit—out of sorts,' she confessed.

'You're not feeling well?' Instantly sympathetic, Miranda had a chair pulled out for her before she could stop her.

But, unable to accept such solicitude when she was not ill, in her rush to say, 'There's nothing wrong with me,' Verity slipped up and added, 'Nothing that seeing one certain person laid flat wouldn't cure, anyway.' And then suddenly, while Miranda looked at her in surprise, it all came tumbling out.

'But your father *promised* you that seat!' Miranda gasped when she had heard it all, her amazement telling Verity that she had truly understood what a shock it had been to have her dreams smashed to smithereens. 'It's yours by right,' added Miranda, knowing all about the firm and how Verity's cousin Basil had been accepted into the company the moment he had finished university.

'That's what I thought,' said Verity glumly.

'And your father must have known how much you wanted it,' said Miranda, incredulous still. 'I know we can all act a bit irresponsibly sometimes,' she added as though, like Verity, she was searching for some reason for that promise being broken, 'but you didn't so much as take one day off from that diploma course you took, and I know for a fact that there were many times you would have liked to have come with the rest of us when we went off for the day somewhere.'

With Miranda commiserating with her, love and loyalty to her father had Verity telling her that she didn't think it was her father's fault that Holt Jepherson had usurped her. And how, in her opinion, the new board member had somehow manoeuvred himself into her rightful place, but how she had vowed to eject him.

'The trouble is,' she concluded flatly, 'that try as I might—and I've thought of little else since it happened—I just can't think of one single solitary way to do it.'

Miranda had no more success than Verity in finding a way for the usurper to be usurped, and when someone else came into the kitchen, in search of ice cubes, Verity pinned a smile to her face and returned with her friend to where the party was in full swing.

Around one o'clock, one or two people started to drift off. But Verity, her thoughts back at Birchwood House where her father's business discussions could still be going on so far as she knew, was in no hurry to go home.

At two o'clock, she was hard put to find a smile when Jolyon became hot under the collar because he thought some man called Vaughan was monopolising her. He had just threatened to punch Vaughan on the nose, when she caught sight of Miranda looking at her and wearing an expression she knew of old. It was Miranda's way of looking when she thought she had just received a brilliant idea.

Extracting herself from the fracas, which fizzled out when the two men had nothing to fight over, Verity went over to where Miranda was standing with Adrian.

'So,' she said, 'are you going to share it?'

'Can you excuse us a moment, Adrian?' asked Miranda, her eyes so brimful of excitement that Adrian, who had seen that look in her eyes before too, murmured:

'God help us all!' and left them to go over and smooth down Jolyon's ruffled feathers.

'You've thought of something?' asked Verity, a shade warily. She had a vague memory that the visit to the disreputable casino had been one of Miranda's less brilliant ideas.

'Have I ever!' Miranda exclaimed, and she was soon launching into, 'How about this . . .'

This, in her view, was another of Miranda's less brilliant ideas. 'You're suggesting I make a play for Holt Jepherson?' she exclaimed when she had heard her out. 'What the dickens would that achieve?'

'You haven't been listening,' complained Miranda, and casting her eyes over to where Adrian was in conversation with the two men Verity had walked away from, 'You've got those two eating out of your hand,' she observed, 'I'm darned sure that Jolyon, and Vaughan too, would rapidly move aside and let you have their place on a board if you asked them.'

Certain that they wouldn't, Verity wondered if this was another occasion when Miranda had imbibed too freely—even if what she had just said brought a reminder that she herself had once said something pretty similar to Holt Jepherson with regard to him and Selene Aston.

But in any case, he was an entirely different kettle of fish from Jolyon and Vaughan, she thought; they just weren't in the same class. By no stretch of the imagination could she see him being taken in by a pair of fluttering eyelashes. Though, not wanting to deflate Miranda, who was only trying to help, she went a little way along with her, in that she replied:

'Holt Jepherson would never go for it—he's too hard-headed. Besides,' she added, not forgetting the sophisticated slinky blonde, 'I don't think I'm his type.'

'He's a man, isn't he?' replied Miranda. And having once seen him, 'And what a man!' But coming swiftly away from her memory of seeing Holt Jepherson at the Country Club that night, 'Why not try it anyway?' she suggested. 'You've got nothing to lose.'

That was true enough. 'I'll think about it,' Verity answered, but she knew she wouldn't. 'Come on,' she said, to get her friend off her pottiest idea yet, 'let's have another drink.'

CHAPTER FIVE

AT four o'clock, Verity left the party. One or two of the revellers were staying on, but by that time she was of the view that she had stayed out late enough. It was her opinion that having been shut out of her father's business discussions, she could safely go home with her intention to show them that she had not wanted to be a part of those discussions anyway, satisfied.

Fifteen minutes later she was tiptoeing up the stairs of Birchwood House, when it came to her to wonder, why on earth was she tiptoeing about the place? This was not the first time that her father had had business discussions with an overnight guest. And if things had followed the normal pattern, then she could be sure that the whisky decanter had been upended many times as the two burnt the midnight oil. By now, she guessed, the pair of them would be sleeping sounder than if they had taken a half dozen sleeping pills.

Miranda's daft suggestion came back to her when in her bathroom, no matter how late the hour, she followed her usual habit of undressing and washing before she slipped her short cotton nightdress over her head.

There would have been no chance of Miranda's not so bright idea working, she thought, even if she hadn't already tipped her hand to Holt Jepherson. He knew full well before she started that she had vowed to take that seat from him.

Visions of that diabolical man seeing straight through her and giving her one of his highly amused glances if she so much as attempted to flutter an eyelash, told Verity that her pride would never stand for such amusement. Anyhow, if he was thinking of asking the slinky Selene Aston to marry him, what chance would she have of cutting her out—even if it was for only as long as it took to get him to do the gentlemanly thing, and step down?

Feeling more depressed than ever, Verity climbed into her bed and put out the light. But sleep was nowhere near as she wished Holt Jepherson joy with Selene Aston, and hoped he would have one gigantic headache in the morning.

She dwelt for some minutes on the man who it went without saying had been treated to every hospitality in her home that night. And she became aggrieved that when she should feel sleepy enough to sleep the clock around, while Holt Jepherson and her father would sleep the sleep of the dead that night, she couldn't summon up so much as a yawn.

Verity was still thinking how every courtesy would be shown to *that man* while he was a guest in her home, and how poor Trudy—who had never seemed poor Trudy before—would most likely have to prod him awake from his whisky-sodden slumber in the morning, when something stirred in her thinking. Some idea was trying to get through!

For a few moments more, not quite sure what idea was in her head waiting to be born, but suddenly aware that after all her searching, something was happening in her ideas department, Verity lay there.

Pushing hard, fear taking her that the idea might fade before she could grasp hold of it, she went back to her thoughts of how always before when they'd had guests in the house, Trudy would awaken them with a tray of tea.

Somehow her thoughts became a jumble, with Miranda's notion of how she should make a play for

Holt Jepherson mingling in with how Trudy was not
backward in coming forward when it came to
reporting to her father, for her own good, it had to be
admitted, any misdemeanour which in her view called
for her to be carpeted. In there too, with her jumble of
thoughts, was the memory of how her father thought
Holt Jepherson's integrity as a business man was
second to none.

Still pushing hard to find her breakthrough, Verity
recalled her father once saying of Holt Jepherson that
he was a man he would trust with his most valued
possession, and suddenly she switched on her bedside
lamp and sat up.

But the excitement that had taken her was
threatening to cloud her thinking, so that she had to
concentrate really hard before she had got it all
together. But pressing determinedly on, get it together
she did. And all at once, alone in her room, Verity
smiled.

Ten minutes later she had gone over what just had
to be her wildest idea to date. But she still could not
find any fault with it, save the nerve it would need for
her to execute it.

She recalled how Holt Jepherson had as good as
dared her to do her worst. And she knew at that
moment that from somewhere, she would find the
nerve required.

She guessed it had been Miranda who had turned
the key to her locked thinking for a way to oust Holt
Jepherson, by suggesting that she should make a play
for him. But it was not him she had to try to impress,
she now saw, but—her father!

He, she knew indisputably, believed Holt to be
utterly trustworthy in business. But what did her
father know of his private life? As far as he knew, Holt
Jepherson could be the biggest rake of all time. And

while her father would not hang him for that, it would be a very different picture, wouldn't it, when in a very few hours from now, Trudy rushed in to tell him how the man he had gone back on his promise to his own daughter for, while a guest in his home, while accepting his hospitality, had, under his very roof, seduced his innocent daughter!

It was too, too sublime, she thought excitedly. She wouldn't be at all surprised to see Monday arrive with one member of the board being booted off it, and the first female ever taking her place.

Verity ignored the dressing gown lying at the foot of her bed when, just before dawn, she left her room and tiptoed along to the room that had been termed the best guest room.

With no sound to be heard other than her suddenly hammering heart, for long minutes she stayed to listen outside the door. Stealthily then, she slowly turned the door handle and pushed the door in a little way. Then, adrenalin rushing through her veins, she took a few moments to steady herself so she could concentrate on the steady even breathing coming from where she knew the bed to be.

As she had thought, Holt Jepherson was out to the world, and, by the sound of it, he would stay that way until Trudy arrived with his tea.

For how long she stood there, just listening to the steady rythym of his breathing, Verity had no idea. But suddenly she was having to scrape together every scrap of her courage to do what had to be done.

That courage was hers when she remembered his, 'You haven't a prayer,' and she recalled that he had actually *dared* her to do her worst. Noiselessly then did she slip inside the room and close the door, and tiptoe barefoot over to the double bed.

Steeling herself, Verity needed to hang grimly on to

that courage in order to reach out to the bed covers. Yet more courage was needed for her to feel to find an opening. But, not so much as daring to breathe a sigh of relief that the fates were with her in that she had, by some great good fortune, come to the side of the bed that appeared to have the most space, inch by furtive inch she took her courage in both hands, and moved from the floor and in between those covers.

Tension kept her rigid when a warmth in the bed told her that Holt Jepherson was much nearer to her than she had supposed. But when suddenly the bedcovers moved and he turned over on to his side, great clamouring alarm bells went off in her head!

Then fear had her frozen! Fear of discovery was keeping her still and cancelling out what would have been an instinctive reaction to catapult from the bed. And, too late to react, by the time her limbs had got release from that spasm of ice-cold fear, Verity found that one of Holt Jepherson's arms was lying across her, and that—too soon—she had been discovered, and not by Trudy, but *by him*!

Yet all was not lost! Rigid as she lay under the bare arm that burned through the thinness of her nightdress, when nothing else happened and Holt made no move to turn on the light to see who he had captured, as her racing heart slowed down to a canter, she heard that his breathing was still rhythmic and that he was still asleep!

Strangely then, when she should have been counting her lucky stars that her plan still had a ninety per cent chance to work, Verity felt anger flare in her that whether Holt Jepherson was carrying a load of Scotch or not, he must be so used to having a woman in his bed that even in sleep it should feel natural to him to anchor a female body to his side.

Stamping down hard on the almost irresistible

impulse to thump him awake and before she went back to her own room to tell him that she was Verity Diamond and not Selene Aston, Verity made herself think only bout how great would be her retribution if she did not give way to the impulse.

Again she listened to his unbroken breathing, but she had to blank her mind off hard as, that bare arm still burning across her, it dawned on her that Holt Jepherson must have got into bed without bothering to don a pyjama jacket, and that, for all she knew, he might have forgotten to bring his pyjamas altogether! And that she *could* be in bed with a man who was stark naked!

Her heart starting to race again in panic, she turned her thoughts to how much more convincing it would be if she flipped back the covers to reveal that bare arm anchoring her to the bed on the moment when Trudy opened the bedroom door. She hoped Holt Jepherson would not again change his position and have his back to her when Trudy arrived. If he stayed the way he was, she thought, with no small degree of relish, intimate was not the word for it!

The first half hour Verity spent in bed with Holt Jepherson dragged interminably. But when in the next half an hour she discovered that, against all odds—though maybe because all through what seemed an age-long night she had not slept a wink—she was on the point of dropping off. She blinked, and was wide awake again.

Trudy should be here soon, she thought. Holt Jepherson's arm was still over her, again bringing thoughts that he hadn't woken because he was so used to being in bed with a female companion. She'd like to bet he would wake up the next time he bumped into somebody during the night, she mused. Trudy, without a doubt, would be going jet-streamed to tell her employer what she had discovered.

But it didn't quite happen that way. For one thing, when she had been positive that she would not nod off again, Verity had fallen into a light doze, and although the sound of the door opening had her coming awake, she had just not got it all together in time to pull back the covers to show the housekeeper how Holt Jepherson had his arm so intimately around her.

Though the rest of her plan was working well, she saw. For by then Trudy, bearing a teatray, was in the room—and her face was a picture!

Scandalised, with her mouth working but with no sound coming out, she looked first at Verity, who stared back solemn-eyed, then, as if believing she had somehow unthinkingly walked straight past the guest room by mistake, Verity saw her look at the other side of the bed. Then, never more shocked, she looked back to her young mistress. Then, without a word but, as Verity well knew, up in arms, she turned about and went smartly out again to close the door behind her with a none too gentle snap.

A smile crossed Verity's features as she overcame her compunction that it could be months or maybe years before she could confess to the kind soul who had nursed her as a baby the truth of the matter. But she had won, she had won! Triumphant, her smile changed to a smirk as the impulse wouldn't be denied to have a look at the sleeping man beside her before her father came roaring in. It was then that Verity received an enormous jolt!

Though jolt did not begin to cover what she felt when, as she turned her head on the pillow, her eyes met full on the wide-awake grey eyes of Holt Jepherson. Stumped for a moment, she had the most disquieting feeling that he had been awake for some time. But, having found herself in sticky situations before, though admittedly, never one like this, she was still glorying in her triumph and was able to dismiss any feeling of disquiet.

Although when she went to sit up, she didn't quite like it that, with his arm still across her, he should sit up too. Half facing him, she did not give him any marks that when he must be fully aware of the situation he was in, he still managed to retain his look of supreme confidence. But she was not of a mind to let him take from her a moment of this glorious feeling of what she had achieved.

She smiled a broad smile when she guessed, although he was covering it well, that he was just too stunned to speak. And she was the first to break the silence, as, 'It would appear, Holt,' she said, almost chrotling in her delight, 'or may I call you Mr Jepherson, that you've forfeited your right to an early morning cuppa.'

With that, she put her hand down to his arm with the intention of removing the offending object from across her person—her father would have heard it all now; there seemed little point in staying.

But oddly, that arm across her was suddenly an iron bar, and was refusing to be lifted out of the way. And she didn't care for it at all that he sounded much too cool, when he drawled casually in reply:

'So it would seem.' And to take her mind completely off the removal of his arm, 'Though I can't say I didn't have a prior warning.'

'You're referring to my telling you I intended to get back what was promised to me?' she questioned, seeing no reason why she should hide behind dishonesty about what her being in his bed was all about—he'd work it out for himself in due time, if he hadn't done so already. But, expecting him to agree that he had meant it was she who had given him prior warning, Verity was puzzled when he shook his head.

'My conversation with your father last evening,' he replied with a pleasant smile, when to her mind he should be scowling like fury, 'was not spent entirely in discussing business.'

'It—wasn't?' she questioned slowly, puzzlement taking some of her triumph away, when she knew full well she still had every reason to feel triumphant.

'I happened to mention that I'd heard a whisper about you not being too happy about my getting a seat on the board,' he enlightened her, causing her to feel not too well pleased that he had discussed her with her parent behind her back.

'Do you usually go in for understatement?' she asked shortly, starting to feel belligerent.

Again he smiled, and she liked that smile no more than she had liked his phoney first smile. 'Clement assured me that you'd come to terms with your disappointment,' he went on. 'Though in taking a father's pride that you're a spirited young woman with a mind of your own, while referring to one or two of your past escapades, he also mentioned, with what I took to be a warning, that there wasn't a trick going which you weren't up to when the mood took you.'

Disgruntled that her father should talk about her, proudly or any other way, to Holt Jepherson, though this was the first she'd heard that her father admired her independent spirit, Verity thought she'd just about had enough of Holt Jepherson. But when again she went to remove his arm from her, she found he had no intention of allowing her to be free. And all at once, when not a fraction would that arm move, she realised that it was not just an iron bar he had placed over her, but a restraining bar!

Hostilely she glanced at him, but her eyes flicked

quickly away when she found that her glance was going down to his broad manly chest to observe its dark contrast of hair. Then, since it did not matter all that much whether she did a disappearing act before her father arrived or afterwards—though he must have been very sound asleep if Trudy was still endeavouring to rouse him—she flicked a lofty look back to her bed companion, and airily she told him:

'So now you know. By now Trudy will have told my father how she came in and found me in bed with you. He'll raise hell,' she said sweetly. And as triumph flooded back at the mighty hell her father would raise—and with Holt Jepherson—she just could not resist, 'You really shouldn't be such a heavy sleeper, Mr Jepherson.'

Again her smile came out. She could afford to smile in her triumph. Even if Holt Jepherson tipped her out of his bed when it dawned on him that her father would be raging in like a mad bull at any moment, she could afford it.

But to have her own smile batted back at her was to have her triumph dipping once again. And that was before, every bit as loftily as she, he thought to tell her:

'At the risk of shattering your illusions, Miss Diamond, I feel it incumbent on me to tell you that far from my being a heavy sleeper, the merest sound can have me awake.' Certain that not even the smallest sound had she made when she had entered his room, Verity was just about to scorn what he had said, when he added, 'For the record, you might like to know that I require very little sleep, and often get by on just a few hours.'

Not wanting to know a thing from that arrogant curving mouth, Verity remembered his steady even breathing, and scorning his lies, challenged:

'You're trying to tell me you were wide awake when I came into your room?'

'Had you left it another two minutes,' he returned unabashed, 'you would have found me with the light on, reading. I thought to read would be a better option than to disturb the whole household by starting my day at such an early hour,' he thought to tell her, while observing with a quirk at the corners of his mouth that, for once, doubt starting to creep in, she had been silenced. 'But,' he went on, when she had still not found her tongue, 'you climbing into bed with me proved an even bigger relief from the boredom of insomnia than a book ever could.'

Amazed at what he was saying, that, if he was to be believed, from the very moment she had opened his door, he had been aware of ... She broke off the thought, her fighting spirit surging up as she roused herself to state coldly:

'I don't believe you.' Memory aided the fight in her when she recalled thinking how, *fast asleep*, he must have thought himself in bed with Selene Aston. 'You'll be telling me next,' she scorned, 'that not only did you know it was me in your bed, but that in seconds you knew exactly what was in my mind!'

'I couldn't think who else it could be,' he murmured sardonically. 'But when I turned over and put my arm across you,' he said, to throw her into confusion that he must have been awake to know that! 'and you showed no sign of wanting to—snuggle up—I had to think again about why I was being so honoured by your visit. It was then,' he added, that phoney smile there again as he ignored the fact that she was fairly spluttering, 'that I recalled your father's timely warning of there not being a trick you wouldn't use if it fitted your necessity.'

'You put your arm around me on p-purpose? To—

to g-gauge my reaction!' Verity was choking on anger that the man she so hated could think she might want to snuggle up close to him. 'Your first thought was that—that I . . .? You didn't!' she denied, trying to get all of one piece. 'You didn't know it was me,' she went on to charge. 'You thought I was Selene A . . .'

'Selene Aston,' he interrupted her smoothly, 'is a totally different armful from you, Verity Diamond.'

Confusion was hers again when she saw his grey eyes go expressively down to where the upper curves of her breasts were showing above her nightdress. Selene Aston, now she came to think of it, while being beautiful, was as thin as a stick!

But that just by the feel of her he had known she was not his blonde girl-friend gave Verity a sudden feeling of distaste. Not that she cared tuppence to know that the *least* he had done with Selene Aston had been to put an arm about her, though she was finding it equally distasteful that the arm that had been around his woman friend was still about her.

'Well, you can just jolly well let go of me now!' she flared. Triumph had gone, and all she wanted to do then was to go back to her own room.

'But, my dear Verity,' Holt objected, 'you came so willingly.'

Damn his eyes, she thought, rendered speechless for a second. 'Well,' she said, dragging up what argument she could find at the truth of his statement, 'you'd just better let me go. My father will be in here at any minute, and . . .'

'Wasn't that what you wanted?' he queried, and looked no more likely to let her go now than he had before as he let it sink in, in case she hadn't already got the message, that Holt Jepherson had seen straight through her brilliant plot within the first minutes of her putting it into action.

But, made to accept that they didn't come much smarter than him, Verity would not let him see how he had shaken her. Her plan could still work, she thought, as she moved her feet to the edge of the mattress.

She had only one thing to say to him then before she loftily took her leave. 'My father will have heard sufficient from Mrs Trueman, without the need to witness me in your—your clutches!' She put her feet over the side of the mattress and pushed with her ribcage against the bar of iron against her—but only to find that she was going nowhere—except nearer to Holt Jepherson!

'Oh no, you don't, little Miss Mischief,' he grunted, and to her utter astonishment, the next she knew was that he had brought his other arm into play, and effortlessly, entirely uncaring that her father could come in at any moment, he had yanked her so that she was close up to him and she was feeling the warmth of his bare skin against her thinly clad hip.

'Let go of me!' broke from her on a flutter of panic.

'Like hell I'll let go of you!' he snarled, and he sounded so tough then that she stared witlessly at him; to see that, his phoney smile gone, he was looking hard-eyed—and ruthless. 'How—with you in my bed, not me in yours—you intended to convince Clement that I've taken such outrageous advantage of his hospitality escapes me,' he gritted, 'unless, that is, you had it in mind to tell him I dragged you from your bed and into mine, to rape you.'

'I wasn't going to accuse you of rape!' she exclaimed, with such honesty as that exclamation left her that some of his anger seemed to evaporate. And still honestly, for all things weren't going according to her plan in that her father was taking an unconscionably long time in getting there, 'I might have done,' she added, 'had I thought of it, but I didn't.'

'Heaven be praised for small mercies,' he muttered. But though his phoney smile had reappeared, she could tell from that glint of steel in his eyes that he was still angry with her. And she was to know fear then when, his look going from her face, his eyes roved to her uncovered shoulders, then moved to linger unhurriedly on her breasts. 'Though if the smallest harm you intended was that I should be branded the vile seducer . . .' he had no need to finish—Verity was on the move.

But her rocket-like movement proved ineffective. For suddenly, Holt Jepherson moving too quickly for her to know how it came to be, she found she was flat on her back, with his chest anchoring the top half of her down. And before she could so much as begin to start yelling, his hands were cupping her face and he was kissing her!

A high-voltage shock went through her as she felt his warm mobile mouth over her own. But when maybe had she been in less of a panic, it might have come to her that her father coming in and finding her fighting Holt Jepherson off would set the final seal to her plan, she was just not capable of any sort of ordered thinking. What she was doing was fighting.

Like a wild thing she pummelled at the hard-muscled arms that were inserted between her arms to prevent her from clawing his face. But she was fighting in vain, for Holt Jepherson was still kissing her.

And his kisses were not limited to just her mouth. Every part of her face was being touched by his mouth, her ears too feeling the touch of his lips, as she pushed her body at him in an attempt to thrust him from her.

'Joining the party?' he queried, with a note of mockery as the lower half of her body pushed violently against him.

How it had come about that the whole of him was lying over her, and not just his chest, she was not stopping to work out. Though perhaps the fact that her feet were coming into play as well as her hands had decided him to limit her movement further.

'Like hell I'm joining the party!' she hissed at the first chance she had when he again took his mouth from hers.

She gave another ineffectual push to his arms, then discovered that it was not arms, but his bare back, and that somehow at some time she had put her arms around him.

'And I thought you liked parties,' he murmured, and kissed her again.

'Will—you—let me—go!' Verity fumed angrily, despite his comment, trying again to push him away with her body, which was about the only weapon she had.

'Why should I?' he returned. But all at once his tone was strangely changed, and he was looking down into her face. 'You're so beautiful,' he whispered, and there was such a contrasting gentleness in him then that it threw her completely.

And it was while her body, hands, and arms were momentarily still, that he kissed her again, only this time tenderly. Verity had still not recovered from being thrown, when that tender kiss transferred from her mouth to trail gently down to her throat.

And when next Holt Jepherson tenderly kissed her mouth, and his hands came to her shoulders in a light caressing movement, Verity knew herself stunned that a man who could be so tough could have such gentle magic in his caress.

Suddenly then, when, had it been a battle of words, she would have fought to the bitter end, all at once, as his mouth again lay over hers in the tenderest of kisses, without her being even aware of it, the fighting spirit that had never been known to fail her was defeated by a feeling that was completely new.

Her hands stayed where they were; around him. And when his hands strayed to caress not only her shoulders, but down towards her breasts, instead of pummelling furiously at that back, she was holding hard on to him. And all tension was to leave her when, on her gasp of pleasured breath, her breasts were captured.

For long minutes Holt continued to kiss and caress her, although by then, fire flickering to life in her, Verity had lost all sense of time. But another gasp was to leave her, when with the low neckline of her nightdress allowing him access, his hands went inside her nightdress and his fingers caressed and teased the naked peaks he had hardened into desire.

A moan of wanting escaped from her when his mouth played over the swollen globes beneath his hands, and her body was pressing against his when his tongue tormented around the pink pinnacle of each breast in turn. And on fire for him, her cheeks flushed with their message of wanting to know more and yet more, Verity clutched him to her and offered to him whatever he would take.

She knew nothing except that she wanted him with all her being, and she was not sure she had not cried out his name. But suddenly, through the headiness of this never-before-known aching need, she became aware that there had been a sound.

Holt had heard it too. For with his body still pulsing vibrantly over her, all at once he had stilled—the sound they had both heard was the sound of a door closing.

Transfixed, she struggled to get out from the vortex of the sensations Holt had wreaked in her, but only one fact of any clearness was to present itself. The fact that, contrary to her previous plotting, she now had no wish for her father to come in.

Tension took her as, too intoxicated by the way he had made her senses sing to think of putting some space between herself and Holt, she turned her head to stare at the handle of the guest room door.

Hardly breathing, she heard her father's footsteps near the door, then pass, then fade away as he went downstairs, and relief poured in.

Though, having gone through a whole gamut of emotions recently, Verity was barely thinking about what happened next, when Holt moved from her. And when she took her eyes from the door and looked back at him, she was astounded to see neither relief nor the desire which she could have sworn he had felt every bit as much as she, but, shatteringly—nothing but sardonic amusement!

Swamped by emotion as she was, she was hardly able to credit that she was again some source of amusement for him. It was then that her pride recieved a kick start. And when only minutes ago she could not have said with any truth that had Holt resumed making love to her, she would have stopped him, her fighting spirit that had been defeated by his lovemaking roared to the surface.

Pride surged in her on an uprish of fury, that while she might still have been putty under his expertise, he was coolly mocking, his expression telling her that what happened now was—precisely nothing.

Her rage white-hot that he had made such a fool of her, Verity bolted to sit upright in the bed. And this time, too enraged to think of counting ten, her hand had swung zooming through the air, and she had the small satisfaction of hearing the crack as her hand found its aim on the side of his face—then she was waiting for nothing.

'What did I do?' came the mocking question behind her as she stormed to the door.

At the door she turned, her eyes sparking out her hate for the man leaning negligently up against the headboard, '*That*,' she hurled across the room, 'was for what you might have done—had I not been so disinclined!'

The mocking laughter that followed her out through the door told her that when it came to letting him know how disinclined she had been—Holt Jepherson knew it the lie of the year.

CHAPTER SIX

BACK in her own room Verity, still furious, went to shower. But when she was under the shower, as her hate for Holt Jepherson spiralled, so an innate honesty turned on her. And she had to face the fact that no amount of water could wash away the memory of how wildly passionate had been the feelings that had overtaken her when she had been in his arms.

It seemed incredible, now she had rid herself of that wanton yearning, that she could act so outside of the person she knew herself to be. It seemed incredible that she could for so much as a split second respond so eagerly to a man she hated so much. She remembered his hands on her breasts and the longing that had taken her. But she also remembered his mockery, his vile mockery; that said that he was aware of every emotion he had wrought in her. Hurriedly she switched her thoughts to concentrate on other, more pressing problems.

It was as plain as day that Trudy could not yet have told her father how only one member of the household had received a cup of tea in bed that morning—and why. Though what Trudy was waiting for, she couldn't fathom, unless ... A glimmer of brightness came into her searchings as she saw that maybe Trudy had thought to spare her father the pain of coming into the guest room and seeing his daughter in bed with his trusted associate.

All was not lost, she thought quickly. A second later, she thought she could safely guarantee that no sooner would breakfast be out of the way than Trudy would be asking her employer if she could see him privately.

Not wanting to miss a moment of seeing Holt Jepherson getting the order of the boot, Verity, intending to be there in the breakfast room to see his face when Mrs Trueman said those magical 'May I see you?' words to her father, hastily dressed and flicked a comb through her hair.

But as she raced downstairs, her footsteps suddenly slowed when it came to her that she would have to verbally lie to her parent when she was called on to tell how Holt had persuaded her into his bed because her bed was only a single one. But fight was again there in her eyes—that seat had been *promised* to her, and that alone meant that the lie was justified.

Expecting to see her father already there, Verity sailed into the breakfast room, then came to a full stop. She had not given a thought to how she would feel to see Holt again; but to see that he was there alone, her father nowhere about, had the memory of what lay between them flushing burning colour to her face, and rooted her in the doorway.

She made an instinctive move to turn and leave, but his mockery as he observed the movement, just as he observed her flare of colour, was to bring all the hate she had for him rising up.

'Not so hungry now?' he murmured, to halt her.

Though before she could come back with any acid, her father had appeared behind her in the doorway to tell her she was blocking the way.

Forced to go forward, Verity took her place at the table and recovered her equilibrium under the cover of her father telling his guest something about being called to the telephone by a friend enquiring if he could play golf tomorrow.

'The early bird catches the worm,' he quipped, it

being well known among his circle of friends that breakfast time was the best time to catch the busy Clement Diamond at home.

Having so far not addressed her parent, Verity was still trying to decide if she should look the picture of injured innocence, ready for what was to come later, or how she should act, when she suddenly sensed her father's eyes on her. Unsmiling, still undecided, she raised her head to look at him.

And she was to send up silent thanks when, taking in the shadows beneath her eyes that revealed that she had done little more than doze in the past twenty-four hours, he remarked, 'You're not getting enough sleep.' His observation, she thought, would augur well for what Trudy had to tell him—that she hadn't, last night anyway, had enough sleep.

But when Clement Diamond went on to confirm that Mrs Trueman had not yet said anything to him—though Verity had already gleaned that from the way he was still treating Holt as an equal and not the louse he was—her father was to make her instantly furious, when, in a good humour obviously, he quipped:

'I suppose you *did* come home last night?'

Angrily, she glared at him that in front of Holt Jepherson he should make it sound just as though she slept around. And she was hating everybody then, that, when none of the men in her set had that much special about them to make her want to go to bed with them, from what her father had said, Holt, with his knowledge of how not too long ago—and without too much trouble—he'd had her responding wholeheartedly to his caresses, must think that she was like that with every man.

But she was not the only one who was out of sorts. For at that moment, saving her from more teasing comment from her father, the door opened and a surly-expressioned Mrs Trueman came in. Holt had already been tucking into bacon and eggs when Verity had arrived, but as Trudy, without a word, thumped fresh coffee down on the table and then, without her usual enquiry to Verity of what would she like to eat, banged rather than placed her toast down in front of her, and, still without saying a word, slammed out. The head of the household, wearing a look of astonishment, turned to his daughter to ask:

'What on *earth's* got into Mrs Trueman?'

Managing to make her expression blank, Verity shrugged, her 'I don't know', of the opinion that while she could have told him exactly what was the matter with their housekeeper, Trudy, truly indignant at what she had found when she'd gone into the guest room that morning, would tell it all so much better.

'Well, we can't have this,' he murmured, with an apologetic look to Holt that he had had to witness such rudeness. 'I'll have a few words with her later,' he said, which had Verity sending a sideways purring glance to the man who in her view had already started down the slippery slide off his board seat, 'and find out what's troubling her.'

'Talking of a few words, Clement,' Holt engaged his host, wiping from his face the amusement with which he had answered Verity's purring look, 'I wonder if I could see you for a few moments before I get off?'

'Of course,' replied Clement Diamond affably. And while at this turn of events all vestige of wanting to purr left Verity, her father added, 'We can go to my study as soon as you like.'

That Holt did not require more coffee, and that her father had eaten all he wanted, was apparent in that before she could think up a thing that would prevent them from having their private *tête-à-tête*, both men had stood up.

She was still furiously searching for a way of stopping them, when with a murmured, and insincere, 'You'll excuse us, I hope, Miss Diamond,' Holt followed her father out.

It could, of course, be some snippet of business which he had overlooked last night about which he wanted a word with her father. But, fuming impotently, Verity knew very well that it wasn't.

Minutes were to tick by as she sat and stared mutinously in front of her. She was hating Holt Jepherson more than ever then, that for a second time he had stolen her thunder. It went without saying that she had said goodbye to that seat on the board, she thought angrily. At any second now her father would be through that door and would be giving her hell.

Moodily she went to the door and opened it to save him the trouble. He was taking longer about it than she had thought, though, and so far she hadn't heard him roar with rage at what she had tried to get away with—*and* with a guest under his very roof! But it was for sure that while he might be controlling his fury in front of Holt Jepherson, when he came to sort her out, she would be hearing him loud and clear.

There would be no mistaking that this time he would carry out his oft-repeated threat to cut off her monthly allowance. And although she came into some money her mother had left her when she reached twenty-five, as her trustee, her father wouldn't let her touch a penny of that either.

Knowing that she was in for a very thin time of it— even Trudy would be against her—stubbornly, Verity was still not regretting what she had done, when she heard the door of the study quietly open, then close again.

But, to her great surprise, it was not her father who came roaring in. And it was not roaring in, but strolling, that Holt Jepherson came.

Though, if he had come to seek her out in order to gloat that as well as getting her into hot, not to say scalding, water, he had just put the kibosh on her last hope of taking her rightful place on the board of Diamond Small Tools, then she was in no mind to take it lying down.

'I suppose you've told my father everything?' she challenged disagreeably.

'You'd prefer he heard it from his housekeeper?' he enquired from his lofty height.

'That means you have,' said Verity sourly, as aware as he was that her father had intended to find out what was troubling Trudy, but certain in her own mind that it had not been from any intention to save him some embarrassment that Holt had got in first.

'I didn't tell him—absolutely *everything*,' he replied, to have hope take an upswing in her that there might yet be something, some way, she could use this to her own advantage and might still be able to get her plan to work. But that was before she witnessed that mockery was back in his eyes. And she was to wish then that she had hit him harder when she'd had the chance, as he added softly, 'For instance, I didn't tell him what a passionate nature you have when your . . .'

'Thanks for nothing!' she chopped him off smartly, a warm pink staining her cheeks.

'Though of course,' he went on, 'I'm sure Clement is aware of your passionate temper.' And as if by an afterthought, coolly he advised, 'He's waiting to see you, by the way.'

'He gave up strapping me years ago,' she snapped, as she pushed back her chair, her pride outraged at the humiliation that it was he who had given her the message that she should go and stand on that bit of carpet.

'I doubt he ever started,' Holt murmured as she

marched past him. 'Which is a pity,' he added, 'because . . .'

'Go to hell!' Verity hissed over her shoulder, and she was across the hall in moments, the door of her father's study in front of her. She paused only to take a deep breath, then she opened the door and went in.

Fully expecting that her parent would not wait to start slamming into her, to her tremendous surprise she saw not a trace of fury in his face as he turned from his speculation of something outside of the window.

'Ah—Verity,' he said mildly. And, when she had thought she would be standing throughout this entire interview, 'Take a seat, my dear,' he added.

Bewildered, for never had she known him to take any of her misdeeds so well, and this her latest and worst misdeed had led her to think he would throw the book at her, Verity was glad to take one of the wing chairs by the fireplace as she sought to find a reason why he was not going for her with both guns blazing.

She was still no nearer to finding that reason when, his expression telling her he was thinking carefully about what he had to say, her father moved from her vision and to the back of her chair.

But it was not until, after a few moments of him saying nothing, he said, 'I'm trying my hardest to be as modern-minded as your generation,' that it dawned on her that the reprimand she had earned must be being tempered by the embarrassment her father must be going through at the subject matter of that reprimand.

Instinctively she made to slew round in her seat. But she checked the movement when it suddenly came to her that she could save him some embarrassment, if he got off his chest what he had to say by addressing his words to the back of her head.

She was still sitting facing the fireplace when Clement Diamond had strung a few of those words together. But, had he gone for her hammer and tongs, it was not certain that she would not, in her defence, have replied with a spirited attack, when he said sadly, 'I can't pretend Verity, that I'm not disappointed in you,' she began to feel more dreadful at his saddened tone than if he had set about her with a whip.

But when she had gone to be feeling too unhappy to think of defending herself, that unhappy feeling was to go hurtling from her, stunned amazement taking its place, when he went on solemnly:

'Holt, of course, has taken the blame upon himself. But . . .'

'*He's* taken the blame!' she exclaimed, startled, jerking halfway round in her seat in her astonishment.

'Of course he has,' her father replied.

Her intelligence for once deserting her, Verity turned back to face the fireplace as she wondered what on earth was going on. Holt had had a first class opportunity to get back at her for what she had intended, and yet, according to her parent, he was somehow taking the blame for the fact that, just before the crack of dawn, uninvited, she had crept into his bed! It didn't make sense.

'Why—er—why,' she asked slowly, 'would he do that?'

'Why, because, despite what's happened, Holt is an honourable man,' he answered, when she needed to have Holt Jepherson's good points re-endorsed like she needed to have acne. 'He has told me,' he quietly added, 'how the two of you lost your heads.'

Her head had shot up at that, but she remained facing the fireplace as she thought—well, she couldn't deny that! There had certainly not been a self-controlling thought in her when Holt had set about

tenderly making love to her. Though, remembering
his cool sardonic amused look after her father had
passed his door, she was equally certain that Holt
Jepherson had remained in full control of his.

But, in accepting that for her part she could not
truthfully argue with her father's statement, though
since it was her part of it that was at issue, she was
about to plead the extenuating circumstances of
wanting that promised board seat for what she had
planned, she was suddenly so shattered, not to say
appalled, by what her father had got in first to say,
that all thought of extenuating circumstances went
from her.

'Naturally, being a man of honour,' said Clement
Diamond, giving her not so much as a hint of
what was to come, 'Holt has told me he'll marry you.
And . . .'

'*Marry me!*'

The two words had left her on a shriek of horror.
That horror was reflected in her eyes as she swung
round in her chair. But she was to see that her father's
disappointment in her went very deeply, because he
was just not seeing, or hearing, her horror, but was
moving from behind her chair, and had gone to
contemplate the view from out of the window.

It was from there that he strove to get over his
disappointment in her. And it was from there that he
resumed, 'I would, of course, have preferred that you
had controlled the attraction Holt has for you, and that
you hadn't lingered to have a word with him when you
came home from your party and bumped into him
looking for something to read in the library. But . . .'

'But . . .' she inserted a but of her own, intending to
get over to tell her parent that it hadn't happened like
that at all, regardless of what tale Holt had told him.
And as for her being attracted to him—*well* . . .!

'But,' he went on, not waiting for her to find the courage she needed to confess 'all', 'even a man of Holt's integrity can't fight his emotions when—er—when they get out of hand.'

That her father was embarrassed again was obvious by the way he choked on a cough, and shuffled his feet. But, while Verity wanted to save him any further embarrassment, she found that she was to feel that self-same emotion of embarrassment when, like a thunderclap, all at once she realised that when she had full proof of how entirely in control Holt had been the whole of that passionate time, somehow he had given her father the impression that their lovemaking had gone further than it had! That, in fact, Holt had let him think that they had been lovers in the full sense of the word!

'Dad, you've . . .' she broke off. You've got it all wrong, she would have said. But, her conscience smiting her that he had got it nearly all right since she wouldn't have had a leg to stand on if Holt had decided otherwise, she swallowed down her denial, and instead told him, as firmly as she could, 'I'm—not going to marry him.'

The long-suffering pained expression that crossed his features told her that where Holt Jepherson's offer to marry her had gone a long way to help ease her father's disappointment, her reply was bringing him fresh disappointment in her. But she was to wish heartily that she had put an ear to the study door to know exactly what had been said while Holt had been with him, for she felt more bewildered than ever when her father sighed, then said quietly:

'I think I know you better than most, my dear. That being so, I don't think you'll deny that it would have to be some emotion stronger than yourself which had you—getting into bed with a man you barely know.'

Pink flooded her face. Put like that, it sounded terrible. But as ever honest with herself, she had to admit that anger had been strong in her, and that hate too had ruled her when she had gone along to the guest room.

'No,' she answered truthfully, 'I won't deny it.'

Clement Diamond smiled to get that admission out of her. But he was to shatter her again, when, that smile still about him, he said gently, 'I know being in love is a very private emotion, darling, but . . .'

Being in love! Hells bells, was he ever wrong! 'I'm not in . . .'

'Stop play-acting, love,' he swiftly cut in. 'There's no need. Holt knows exactly how you feel about him.' She rather thought—given that her chemistry had gone along a road she had not considered possible when he had aroused her to desire—that she had left Holt in no doubt how she felt about him. 'And so,' her father was going on, 'do I. It was love at first sight that took you, wasn't it?'

Vigorously shaking her head when her voice proved to be in shock from hearing the way her father was choosing to see things, when Verity did find her voice, it was to hotly deny anything of the sort.

'Love him?' she exclaimed heatedly. 'I ha . . .'

'You're being your usual stubborn self, I can see,' she was cut off, his tones severe for the first time since she had entered his study. And his face was as stern as his words, when he told her sharply, 'Here you have a man, whom you must think something of to have done what you did; a man who's willing to get you out of the compromised position in which Mrs Trueman found you this morning; yet still you're being argumentative!'

'You sound as though you want me to marry him,' said Verity, digging her heels in when he wouldn't let her get it across that she didn't care one iota for Holt, and every bit as stubbornly as she had been accused of being, 'Why?' she asked, following up that question when it looked as though he was going to duck it, 'Is it because you can't stand the thought of Trudy going around with a long face if I—if we,' she amended, 'don't do the—as she would term it—the decent thing?'

'Mrs Trueman has every right to be upset,' she was told sternly. 'She must have had the shock of her life when she . . .'

'But it isn't that, is it?' questioned Verity, her intelligence waking up at last from the bombardment of the one shock after the other it had received—starting with the moment when things had started to get out of hand when Holt Jepherson had so tenderly kissed her. 'What hold has he got on you?' she asked. And seeing his start of surprise, she knew she had been on the right track all along to think that somehow Holt Jepherson had used trickery to get her seat on the board. 'Is he blackmailing you about . . .'

'Blackmailing me?' His face was such a picture of astonishment, she just had to know that however Holt had managed to get her father to break that promise to her, it had not been by the use of blackmail.

'If it isn't that, then it's something just as vile,' she stated, her anxiety for him suddenly overtaking her horror at the suggestion that Holt Jepherson intended to marry her. 'Oh, Dad,' she said softly, 'can't you tell me?'

'There's nothing to tell,' he replied, every bit as stubborn as she could be at times, as she very well knew.

'I don't believe that,' she said, staying quietly in there, determined, now she had got started, to know all that there was to know. 'Just as you want me to believe that Holt Jepherson is a man of his word, so I believe that you too are a man of your word. And yet,' she pressed on, 'when you *knew* full well what it meant to me to be a part of Diamond's, you broke that solemn promise you made to me when I was eighteen.'

'I . . .' he said, and Verity held her breath. She wanted more than just that 'I'. That night when he had first broken the news to her, their voices had risen in argument. But they were not raising their voices now, and she sensed that he was very near to telling her the truth of why that promise had been broken. 'I—had to—break it,' he said at last. 'I didn't want to, but I had no other choice.'

To hear him say he had not wanted to break his promise gladdened her heart, and warmed her through and through. But her love for him was uppermost just then; and aggression against Holt Jepherson for the hold he must have on her dear parent was to rise up within her.

'Just what trickery did he use to get you to break that pro . . .'

'Trickery?' interrupted Clement Diamond, looking totally amazed to hear her use that word. 'There was no trickery,' he told her sharply. But in the throes of overcoming his amazement, he had her looking at him wide-eyed when, as if forgetting she was there, he muttered, 'Had it not been for Holt, Diamond Small Tools would have collapsed.'

'Coll . . .! What are you talking about?' she gasped, and her shock caused him to collect himself and to realise what he had just said.

'I—hadn't—intended you to know,' seemed to be dragged from him.

'Why not?' Stunned, again she was seeking answers, but she just could not believe any of what she was hearing.

But she hadn't heard the half of it, she was to discover, for her father, after looking discomfited, decided to answer her question, and told her:

'Pride, basically, I suppose. My pride—your pride; you've always been so proud of what I've achieved; my pride that I didn't want you to know that the firm I'd slaved to get started looked to be going to go under unless I could do something about it.'

Go under! Winded to hear such a statement, Verity just stared. 'But,' she protested, her memory surfacing, 'you have order books that are overflowing. You told me so yourself only a couple of . . .'

'We have,' he agreed, which in no way made things any clearer for her. 'But,' he said, seeing her confusion, 'as you probably know, most firms are run on bank overdrafts.'

'Yes,' she agreed, 'I know that.'

'What you don't know,' he enlightened her, 'is that to obtain those full order books, I had to take the risk and make a colossal investment in new machinery. The showdown came,' he went on, 'when the bank called a halt to a further loan.'

'But what did you need a further loan for?' she asked, having been with him until then.

'Materials,' he said briefly. 'I had all the new machinery I wanted to match my competitors who were after the same orders, but I had no money to buy the materials with which to produce the goods.'

'I have some money,' Verity said promptly, eager to let him have every penny. 'You're my trustee. I needn't wait until I'm twen . . .'

'I'm talking about real money,' he turned her offer down gently. 'The money your mother left you wouldn't begin to get us out of the red.'

Verity was silent as it struck her that if the money she would come into in four years time did not even begin to scratch the surface of what her father required, then he must have gone searching high and low for someone to back him who did have the kind of money he was looking for.

'Holt Jepherson has real money?' she asked, the fact that he had agreed to do the 'decent thing' and marry her long gone from her mind.

Her father nodded to confirm that Holt had backed him. 'I was lucky that he was on the look-out for a good investment at the time,' he said. 'Though naturally, I couldn't expect him to chip in with such a vast amount and not want to keep a finger on the pulse of how the business was being run.'

'He demanded a seat on the board?' she enquired, but, for the first time when that prized seat came under discussion, there was no heat in her.

'I offered it to him, Verity,' he said. And telling her exactly how it was, 'Diamond's employ hundreds of people, I didn't have only you to consider.'

It was from that statement—that statement that he did not have only her to consider, that Verity was to see how this man who had always given her everything she had ever wanted, must have grieved that through force of circumstance, he had had to withhold from her something he knew she wanted above all else. She remembered the look of strain that had been with him not too long ago, and she felt dreadful that while he must have been nearly out of his head with worry, she had gone her own sweet way, untouched by any of it.

Suddenly choked, all sign of rebellion left her that while she had been as happy as a lark, there must have been countless nights when he had lain awake searching for a way to not only save the firm of Diamond Small Tools, but also the jobs of all those people he employed.

'I wish you'd told me before,' she said when she

thought she could say anything without bursting into tears. It was no help to recall how offhandedly she had treated him in those early days after he had broken his solemn word. But she was to feel more terrible than ever when, in an attempt to tease, he said:

'I expect I can be as stubborn as you when my pride is affected!'

Verity kept back her tears, just. But there was an immense difference in the girl who had gone into the study expecting to get her head bitten off, from the subdued and thoughtful young woman who came out.

She had climbed the stairs and had gone into her room without realising that she had done so. But, as she caught sight of her bed, and aware suddenly that she felt dog tired, there was too much buzzing around in her head for her to think of trying to catch up on some of the sleep she had missed.

In the next minute or so she had collected a jacket from her wardrobe and, from habit, her shoulder-bag, then she went back down the stairs.

The tall figure of Holt Jepherson appeared from nowhere when she reached the bottom of the stairs, and that he stood blocking her way caused her to stop and to look up at him.

But so downcast was she feeling just then that even though there was blatant mockery in his eyes as he asked a sarcastic, 'Forsaking me for the lovelorn Robey?' the charge of aggression that had always been in her for this man just refused to spark. And it was quietly, a seriousness there in her face, that she shook her head, and told him:

'I'm going for a walk.'

She lowered her eyes aware that he was quietly studying her. And when he did not step aside to let her pass, she guessed she was in for some more of his mockery. But she was to feel a dart of surprise, when his voice level, and without a trace of mockery he asked softly.

'Want company?'

Verity shook her head. Somehow just the softness of his tone had triggered off in her a feeling of again wanting to burst into tears. But her pride was saved, in that after a pause, without saying another word, Holt stepped to one side. She did not thank him, but went swiftly forward and out through the front door.

CHAPTER SEVEN

THE jumble that had been in her head when she had left the house was still much of a jumble a half an hour later as Verity trudged along the country roads and lanes around Lower Bassett.

But as she went over and over all her father had said about the terrible worrying time he'd had, gradually the shock of just why his promise to her had been broken began to wear off. And with that shock receding, so as she trudged on, did her thoughts first begin to flit, and then to linger, on what else he had said at that interview—that interview which would never have taken place had she herself not started it all by getting into bed with Holt Jepherson!

Whether it was because it was now daylight and not dark as it had been when she had hatched her little plot, or whether it was because the sobering news her father had recently imparted had shocked some common sense into her, she was too confused to know. But what she did know was that, in that broad daylight, the idea that had in the early hours seemed little short of illustrious, now seemed to her to be little short of appalling.

Hastily she chased away thoughts that would have encroached on how mindless of anything and everything she had been when Holt had put himself out to get her to respond. She had more than enough confusion to cope with, wondering why on earth he had told her father he would marry her, without having to handle the mass of confusion that would ensue if she paused to try to analyse any of that totally out-of-control person he had made of her.

Turning into another lane, she was certain that Holt's offer to marry her had not been seriously meant. But by the time she had reached the end of that lane she had remembered how much store her father set on the new board member's integrity.

Her head starting to spin, as she ploughed on, Verity asked herself, could she—with her father's trust in everything Holt did and said being so implicit— could she really be so very certain that his offer to marry her had not been seriously meant?

Her thoughts hopped back to remember it had been his concern for her father that had seen him calling that evening to tell her that her parent had earned his rest when he came home. And recalling the fright she had received that her father might be ill, she realised that Holt had called because he was aware of the great strain her father had been under, in trying to find a backer—a backer whom he could trust!

Hot on the heels of that thought, she was recollecting how Holt had not given away to her parent the full extent of how badly she had behaved. Obvious to her then, she saw that it was to save him strain of another sort that Holt had tempered down the truth to make it look as though they had bumped into each other when he'd been looking for something to read, and that from the library, their emotions beyond their control, they had gone to his bedroom.

'Oh God!' she groaned out loud, wading ankle-deep in confusion. Holt must have thought that by keeping the truth from him, he would save him the fresh worry that he might have a promiscuous tramp for a daughter.

With her thoughts skipping backwards and forwards between Holt and her father, Verity, getting bogged down in the quagmire of her thoughts, was able to see only one thing with any clarity. And that was, with her father so recently near to despair with his business worries, how could she, when he had sounded so keen that she should marry Holt, now go back home and tell her father that not only was she not going to marry him, but cause such embarrassment to his pride that he might never be able to look Holt in the eye again, by confessing that she had—without the smallest encouragement—gone along to the room allocated to his honoured guest and climbed into bed beside him?

Her head starting to pound, she knew then that she loved her father too much to relieve her guilt by confessing anything to him until she had got it all a bit straighter in her mind. Though since her watch showed she had been out for ages and had been able to come to no conclusion other than that she did not want her father to know another moment of worry, she saw that things were just not going to become any clearer until she had gone back home and had found out exactly what Holt had meant by saying he would marry her.

Tiredness, not to say a reluctance to have to seek out Holt to ask him about his marriage proposal, made her push her feet in the direction they had to go on that return journey. What on earth she did if he did say he was serious, she just didn't know, but the way she felt then, it wasn't her that had to be protected, but her father.

'Hello, Trudy,' she said, forcing a smile in an endeavour to break through the housekeeper's chilly exterior as she entered the back way in through the kitchen door.

Silence was her greeting. But although it had been brought home to her how very much in the wrong she had been, having had her olive branch rejected, there was just too much pride in Verity to make her offer another one.

'Have you any idea where Mr Jepherson might be?' she enquired, unable to prevent the slight tilt to her chin, although her question was politely asked. Though she had to bend when, alarm suddenly hitting her that he might have left, 'He's still here, isn't he?' she asked quickly.

'You might try looking in the best guest room,' Mrs Trueman answered stiffly.

Verity thanked her, but knowing Trudy's dry tongue at times, she knew darned well that she had only just managed to bite back on an acid, 'You know where it is, I believe.'

There was no sign of her father when Verity went along the hall. And as she went up the stairs in search of Holt Jepherson, she was glad about that. To her way of thinking she had to get this marriage thing sorted out first, and from there she could set her course on just how little, or just how much, she should tell him.

Holt Jepherson looked up when, without knocking, she entered his room. But, when her tongue froze and she could not find a way to get started, just as if he was used to some female coming into his bedroom at any odd time of the day, he, having no word for her either, did no more than calmly carry on re-packing his overnight bag.

Needing some help to get started, Verity found it not the slightest help to be ignored just as though she was not there. She aimed a look of dislike at his back, and just to show that the uncommon occurrence of being ignored mattered not a jot to her or her pride, she opted to take her casual ease in one of the bedroom chairs.

So it was that when Holt straightened from completing his task, it was to observe that Verity was sitting with her long legs stretched out in front of her,

her hands bunched moodily in her jacket pockets, and that she was wearing a stubborn look that said, for all this interruption was none of his making, she would be damned if she would speak first.

Eyeing him from the silence of her chair, Verity could have sworn she saw a corner of his mouth twitch, just as though he was having the devil's own work not to burst out laughing. But doggedly she stuck in there, words having to be said between them before he left, even if she did not care very much that again, apparently, she had caused him some amusement.

But her stubbornness was rewarded in that Holt *was* the first to speak. Though she was forewarned by the light that came to his eyes as he moved to stand casually against a chest of drawers that anything he said would be accompanied by mockery.

'To what,' he enquired with a lift of his right eyebrow, 'do I owe the privilege of *this* visit?'

As tired as she felt, Verity experienced a dart of aggression. But, realising suddenly that she would get nowhere if she pitched in with a few insolent comments of her own, she swallowed her ire. Though she could not refrain from favouring him with a glowering look when, as evenly as she could, she replied:

'Relax, Jepherson, I'm not up to anything.'

Levelly, he looked at her for several moments, but mockery was still there, not to mention a trace of sarcasm to accompany his sceptical:

'Reformed while we were out, were we?'

Glaring at him, Verity moved her feet moodily. But having found her voice, the words needing to be said were there trembling on her lips, although it was a mite belligerently that, bunching her hands deeper into her pockets, she said:

'Word has it you want to marry me.'

With what her visit *this* time was all about now out in the open, she did not like one tiny bit that she was made to suffer another scrutiny. A longer scrutiny this time, as mockery went from his eyes, and no hint of a smile was to be seen on his mouth. Then, quite bluntly, he was telling her:

'You appear to be misinformed, Miss Diamond.' And while her eyes shot wide and were fixed to his, he added coldly, to set her straight, 'I never, at any time, stated that I wanted to marry you.'

'But you told my father . . .' she began rapidly, only for her voice to fade in her sudden confusion when, obviously not seeing that she wanted a serious discussion, Holt turned from her and appeared to be searching for something on the chest of drawers behind him.

But she was to have his attention again when the cufflinks he must suddenly have realised had not been put into his luggage were retrieved from the chest top and slipped into his trousers pocket. For it was then, as he faced her again, that he drawled casually:

'My recollection of what I told your father was not that I wanted to marry you, but that marry you I would.'

Something hot and sarcastic sprang to her lips, but again she fought down the comment which would get her nowhere in her quest to get something together for when she next saw her parent.

'My father said you were an honourable man,' she said instead. But she was unable to keep the edge from her voice when she questioned, 'You would agree to marry me—obviously against your natural inclination—just because it appears you've compromised me while a guest in his home?'

'That—plus a few other reasons,' he replied coolly.

'Mrs Trueman,' she guessed, not believing it. But, niggled by him, though she was sure it had nothing to do with the fact that he was making it plain that he could think of many things he would prefer than to have to marry her, her aggression refused to stay down as she told him haughtily, 'Well, don't give our housekeeper another thought Mr Jepherson. I've suffered Trudy's black looks before, and surv . . .'

'You're in the habit of hopping into bed with every male guest your father invites home?' he chopped her off sharply, making her catch her breath at the speedy and sudden conclusion he had drawn from what she had just said.

She sent him a look of dislike for his gall, but she was as quickly on top to toss at him, 'You were the first,' and, acid creeping in, 'It's put me off that particular idea for life!'

Her acid, she saw, didn't so much as dent him. For his voice was silky with mock charm when he came back, 'It would appear I've achieved something, be it only that Clement's future overnight guests may rest safely in their beds.' And batting off unconcernedly that her look of dislike had changed to one of hate, his eyes had suddenly narrowed, and his tone was once again tough, when he said shortly, 'Another adventure of the same sort could have a very different ending.' And, his aggression all at once unleashed, 'Good God, woman,' he barked, 'didn't you give a thought to what could have happened?'

Objecting strongly to being thought brainless, Verity had to own that she had not, possibly because she had always felt safe in her home, given the smallest thought to the notion that harm could befall her while her father was just across the landing.

'No, I didn't,' she snapped angrily, honestly.

'You thought your look of innocence would protect

you!' he scoffed. And aggressive still, he positively thundered, 'Where the hell have you been, that you haven't realised that not every man will stop when he has you willing?'

It had been from her father that Verity had expected to have her ears singed. And it was not at all to her liking that it was Holt Jepherson who had taken it upon himself to do the roaring.

'I don't respond like that with every man!' she yelled right back. 'And I . . .' Suddenly she hesitated, his remark about her look of innocence, added to his remark about him stopping when he had her willing, merging as one and causing her curiosity to get the better of her, so that she just had to ask, 'Was it because you realised I was a virgin that you stopped— er . . .?' She hesitated again, her question getting confused when she saw he was looking little short of poleaxed. 'You—didn't know—did you?' she asked faintly.

Her answer, when he had recovered from looking completely stunned, was there in the full force of his wrath. 'My *God*!' he fairly bellowed. 'You're not safe let loose! Don't you *know* the risk you ran getting into bed with me like that?'

'Of course I *know*,' she flared angrily, not thanking him if he thought it was up to him to tell her the facts of life. 'But I wouldn't have let you . . .' She damned him, as she damned the searing hot blush that rushed to her face as she recalled how mindless of anything she had been in his arms.

'You *would*! You know damn well you would. Had not the closing of your father's door reminded me that as a guest I owed him the courtesy of not ravishing his daughter, you would have been mine by now, and you can't deny it!'

Having thought she had sufficient honesty in her

soul to be able to shame the devil, suddenly Verity knew that this she could not take. Unable to admit to him the truth of what he was saying, and at that moment taking no solace from the fact that from what he had said she could glean that he had been nowhere near as cool as he had appeared that moment before she had hit him for his trouble; she abruptly left the chair she had been lounging in, and went quickly to the door.

But at the door, she was glad to feel a modicum of composure returning. And though slight, it was of sufficient quantity for her to be able to drawl an airy, offhanded:

'See you around some time, Jepherson!'

She was about to turn the door handle when his quiet reply of, 'Like—in church?' had her spinning round, her airy, offhand manner nowhere to be seen, as, confused again, she stammered:

'But—but I thought—you didn't w-want to marry me?'

Aggression had gone from him, she saw, but all the arrogance in the world was his, as he shrugged loftily, 'I don't. But I will.'

'*You* will!' Staggered by his cool statement, she had taken several paces back into the room before she found enough wit to challenge, 'You sound—as though you think I'd *agree* to such a thing?'

Arrogant wasn't the word for it when, with a wealth of confidence, Holt told her, 'You, Verity Diamond, don't have any choice.'

His colossal confidence made her hesitate again, but it was only for a moment. Then she was there again to challenge, 'You know something I don't?'

Holt smiled that smile she had seen before, but which she did not like any better now than she ever had. 'I know,' he answered her smoothly, 'that despite you being something of a head-case, and more than capable of acting without thought to the consequences to get what you want, the love you have for your father comes first.'

She was as enamoured by being called a head-case about as much as she was enamoured that he had seen her Achilles' heel. But, since he knew that much, and since she hadn't a clue what he was getting at, there seemed to be only one way of finding out more.

'You're trying to tell me something?' she suggested casually.

'There's not much more to tell, is there?' he commented. 'I learned a short while ago that Clement has told you how Diamond Small Tools would have gone under if he hadn't been able to find someone to finance him.'

From that Verity had a suspicion that Holt would never have told her about the company's dire financial position had her father, while she was out on her walk, quite obviously, not told him she knew. Though tiredness was starting to grab at her to confuse what it was he was trying to tell her, suddenly it struck her that even when she had been calling him names, Holt had not so much as breathed a word that the firm would crumple without his backing, and that for him to refer to it now must mean that it had something to do with what they were discussing. It was then that she began to sense a threat that he was referring to it at all!

'Your backing,' she said swiftly, 'that money,' she added, panicking when she thought of the massive load of worry not having that backing had been for her father. 'It is all signed and sealed, isn't it? I mean,' she went on rapidly, more panic flooding her that for Holt to have had business discussions with her father last night could mean that there was still some doubt about that backing, 'you have had some sort of legal contract drawn up and . . .'

'Drawn up, and signed, and sealed,' he interrupted when she would have gone spurting on. But his next words were to do nothing to allay her sudden panic, for with that smile she didn't like appearing again, he thought to mention pleasantly, 'Though of course, it did occur to me to have an escape clause inserted into that contract.'

Too late Verity realised that she had taken on a man who was even trickier than she would have believed when she had thought to cross swords with him. And she blamed her lack of sleep that the only reason her grey matter could come up with for him mentioning that escape clause was that it somehow tied up with him saying he would marry her. She shook her head as though that would clear it. But she still had no brighter thought when she asked quietly:

'Are you saying that—if I don't agree to marry you—you'll use that escape clause?'

Her answer was in the shape of a question. But, his smile gone, that question told her all she needed to know when, his eyes fixed on her tired eyes, Holt asked:

'Don't you think your father has had more than his fair share of worry just lately?'

So he *did* intend to marry her! Aware that she had thought herself confused before, Verity was of the opinion that if that had been confusion, then she just did not know what she was in the middle of now. Though quite clear was the fact that, when once she would have clapped her hands at the thought of Holt Jepherson moving over to make way for her to have that seat she had so wanted, if it was to be a choice between that seat and her father being snowed under with worry again—as Holt had said, she just did not have a choice.

Though not thrilled with the idea of being shackled to him for life, she sought round to see if there was any way in which she could get out of it.

'What about Selene Aston?' she asked with sudden life; with the air of a conjuror pulling a rabbit out of a hat. 'I thought you were near enough engaged to her?' Her ray of hope was shortlived.

'Did you?' He seemed surprised and, she observed, a past master at non-answers. Though he was to serve her with more confusion when he remarked, 'I noticed . . .' a hint of devilment had come to his eyes as, '. . . in bed this morning,' he inserted, 'that you weren't wearing an engagement ring. Do I take it there's no one else you want to marry?'

Verity recalled telling him last night that she would show him her engagement ring when she got home, and she shook her head. But before she knew it, she found that honesty had tripped her up in that, quite without thinking, she had mumbled:

'Nobody ever made me feel the way you did this morning.'

She wished the words back as soon as she had realised what she had said. But, contrary to her expectation, Holt did not come back with something sarcastic, or gloat, but, as if he understood how she was feeling, he asked gently:

'Bewildered you, has it, Verity?'

She observed that his expression had softened, and that honesty was still with her as, 'Some,' she replied, though she wondered if she would ever be free of bewilderment of one sort or another. She was still trying to get free of it, when, returning to what so incredibly was the subject under discussion, 'This marriage,' she said, still trying to find a way out of it, 'are you planning a name only thing—if I agree, I mean,' she thought to add quickly, 'or,' she said, starting to wish she had walked straight past the guest room door without stopping, 'or is it a—full marriage—you have in mind?'

'You have some special reason for wanting to hang on to your virginity?' he queried, the sarcasm she had expected a moment ago, there in his reply.

But her question had been answered, even if she felt too mixed up to know for sure what she thought that, should any marriage take place between them, Holt would settle for nothing less than a marriage in every sense.

More than a little fed up, aware that his eyes were watching her, she moved over to the window. Her fingers absently played with the window catch as she searched to find something, no matter how insignificant it might be, that would make a match between the two of them make some sense to her. But when, as if knowing the confusion she was awash with, Holt kept silent and gave her as many minutes as she needed to sort something out, all she could come up with was:

'This is all wrong.'

She had not turned from the window, though she was seeing nothing of the splendid view. But when Holt was neither denying nor agreeing about the rightness of what had been proposed, but left it to her to tell him exactly what she thought was wrong with the idea, her fingers came away from the window catch, and she turned round to tell him:

'I don't even like you—I don't think,' even whether she liked him or not suddenly confused in her head. 'And you can't like me,' she went on quickly, though she was glad she could be clear in her head about that. For remembering how she had acted with him from the very first, she could safely assume that there had been nothing about her to stir anything but loathing in him.

Her eyes flickered to him—not that she expected

him to disagree and tell her that like her he did, she would not have believed him anyway. But, reluctantly, she was to give him credit that he was not resorting to being dishonest with her, in that he shrugged aside their mutual dislike, and, just as though the little regard they had for each other had nothing to do with the issue, told her bluntly:

'When it comes to your father's peace of mind, not to mention the certainty of the business going to ruin, you'd marry me, and you know you would.'

It disconcerted her that this man whom she wasn't sure she had any liking for should know her that well. Of course he had seen her love for her father—it must have been there out in the open that time he had called when she'd panicked and had urgently asked him what was wrong with him. And of course he was right, head-case though he thought her, but even if she lived to regret it afterwards, then yes, to rid her father of more stress when he was of an age to be in the coronary belt, she could see herself marrying Holt to save her father, and to save for him his pride and joy, Diamond Small Tools.

But when possibly she might have confirmed there and then that there was little she would not do for her much loved parent, suddenly her natural intelligence was pushing through the fog of her tiredness. Then it was that while she could see all the reasons why *she* might have to marry him, hanging grimly on before weariness fogged her brain over again, she sought to examine his reasons for saying that *he* would marry her.

'Just what are you up to?' she asked sharply, the sharpness of her tone as much as the unexpected question, she thought, responsible for his look of surprise.

'Up to?' he queried, his surprise gone, his

expression giving away nothing of what was going on behind his forehead.

'Oh, come now, Holt,' said Verity, glad to feel alive again and putting it down to the shock of all that had happened that she hadn't attempted to get to the bottom of all this before now. 'Smarter than me you may be,' she allowed, 'but I'm not so dumb that I'll swallow this sudden notion you have to lead me up the aisle, without wanting to know what you get out of it.'

'Did I say you were dumb?' he enquired. 'I have every respect for your intelligence.'

'You called me a head ...' She broke off, aware that, still smarting from what he had called her, she had let herself be sidetracked, and that she had just received yet another of his non-answers to a question. 'You don't want to marry me any more than I want to marry you,' she resumed hotly. 'And I just can't see it mattering a damn to you what sort of a glowering expression our housekeeper wears, or for however long she wears it!' She came to a stop, but she was still searching as, speaking her thoughts aloud, she pushed on, 'It can't be that you're out to get the chairmanship of the company, or you'd use that legal escape clause you spoke of anyway and stay to be around to pick up the pieces when the company collapsed ...'

'Smart girl,' Holt congratulated her quietly. 'I have more than enough to occupy me with my other concerns than to want to be the chairman of another.'

The fog was coming down again, another of his sidetracking comments again putting her off her course. 'So tell me,' she gave up. 'And don't insult my intelligence, the intelligence you say you have every respect for, by using me—you—being compromised, as a reason for saying you'll marry me.'

Her eyes on him, Verity, already irritable in her

weariness, saw the serious expression with which he was observing her suddenly change. But when the confusion and frustration in her in not being able to find the answers she wanted had brought her temper very near to fraying, she exploded completely over the top when Holt's serious expression was replaced by a huge grin.

His mockery at that stage was something which she just could not handle. Nor, when she knew full well that he could barely stand the sight of her, could she handle the way, only just holding in a laugh, she would swear, in which he placed his hand over her heart and declared:

'It could be that I've fallen—er—base over apex in love with you.'

It was just too much. At the end of her tether, hurt took her then, and his mocking action, his mocking words, were more than she could take. 'Damn you!' she shrieked, and unable at that moment to stay in the same house with him, let alone the same room, like a streak of lightning, she was off.

Hurtling down the stairs, she was not conscious of finding her car keys as she went. But in seconds she was out to her car still parked out on the drive where she had left it when she had come home from the party; and with tyres screeching a protest, she was away. Emotions which had been torn apart in her, starting with when Holt had released the spring of the passionate woman that had lain dormant in her, were just too much to be coped with.

Some inner subconsciousness had her aware that she was out on a main road, but when it came to her that she was shaking too violently to be in charge of a car, Verity turned off into a minor road and after a few minutes turned into a narrow, seldom-used lane, and pulled up halfway down it.

For all of ten minutes, she was incapable of more than bitty thought. Never, she realised, had she ever been so furious in her life as when she had heard Holt Jepherson, his loathsome mockery there, telling her that the sky would fall in before he would ever come to love her. Telling her, hand on heart, that he would marry her because it could be that he loved her. She half wished then that she had stayed to tell him he was the last person she would ever fall in love with either.

Gradually she began to get herself together again. But while she could see that, bogged down by endless confusion which no matter how hard she tried to climb out from, only enmeshed her deeper and deeper—and she saw that the confusion of the last hours was the reason for her taking off the way she had—she was still no nearer to finding out why she should feel so hurt at Holt Jepherson's final remark. It was for sure that it didn't matter a hoot to her that he would never love her.

She ousted him from her mind with the thought that he had probably left Birchwood House by now, the clock in her car showing that it was as near to lunch time as made no difference. Though she sighed that she couldn't be certain that with lunch about to be brought to the table, her father would not persuade Holt to stay to lunch. That she had no wish to see that mocking devil again settled the matter of whether she should return home to lunch.

Tiredness again invaded her as she adjusted her position in her car. Inside minutes her head had begun to nod. Her thoughts had just drifted to remember how the last time she had screamed out of the drive the way she had, that her father had exploded; when she sank further down in her seat.

She was on the point of hoping that her father had

neither seen nor heard her departure, for one way and another she appeared to have enough problems without being read the Riot Act when she arrived home, when sleep claimed her.

CHAPTER EIGHT

IT was dark when Verity awakened from her exhausted sleep, and for a moment she did not know where she was. But when she moved to change her stiff position and her hands came into cold contact with the leather of the car seat, everything came rushing back.

She came rapidly wide awake then, and saw with amazement that she had been asleep for hours. Although when she got down to thinking about it, she saw that perhaps it wasn't so amazing. Her body had needed to rest, not to mention that she had been brain-weary into the bargain.

Aware that she was starving, she had put on the car headlights and had started up the car with the intention of going home, when she suddenly changed her mind.

She groaned as it hit her that she still hadn't any idea what she was going to say to her father if he again alluded to the ludicrous idea that she was going to marry Holt Jepherson.

But she had a small respite when she recalled that her father would be out playing Bridge tonight. Though with Holt gone, and her father out, the thought of going home to a none too communicative Trudy had Verity deciding that of the lesser evils, she would eat in town.

She was midway through her meal when she put her knife and fork down, and came to the conclusion that she was not as hungry as she had thought. But home and Trudy having no more appeal than they had before, she ordered a pot of coffee and, when sipping a cup, she realised that while she had never felt so lonely in her life, that she had no wish to call up any of her friends or, if they were out, track them down and join them.

She was on her second cup of coffee when, her thoughts back with her father and Holt, she was again beset by worry. It was all very well, she found, to dismiss this marriage idea as ludicrous, but having come off the worst when she had tried to put one over on Holt, she was not at all sure of her chances not to push him to use that escape clause if she said she wouldn't marry him.

For some minutes she mutinied against him as she wondered about the integrity in him which her father so respected. To her way of thinking there couldn't be all that much integrity in Holt when, if he didn't get his own way, he would ruin her father by using that escape clause, even if it was a perfectly legal clause.

Though still thinking about that word integrity, Verity found she was getting bogged down again when she considered it was only because of his honour that he had said he would marry her anyway. And that just had to mean he was all the honourable things her father had said he was, didn't it? For any other man would not have taken the blame as he had, and would not have agreed he had compromised her, but would have made no bones about telling her father, regardless of the welter of embarrassment he would suffer, that it hadn't been in the library that he had come across her, but that he had first become aware of her presence when, uninvited, she had climbed into his bed.

Verity was on her third cup of coffee and recalling how she had thought that, even if she lived to regret it, to save her father from more worry, and ultimately, save for him the company that was his life, she must marry Holt, when, like a bolt from the blue, it suddenly hit her that, when several of her male friends were what could be termed wealthy, not for a moment could she consider marrying any one of *them*!

It was at that point that she left the restaurant and headed home. She had no idea what that last little revelation had all been about, because she *liked* her friends, but she had had enough of confusing thoughts, and even Trudy seemed a better proposition than another dose of clogged-up, mixed-up thinking.

But, in her assumption that her father was out playing Bridge, and that Holt Jepherson had long since left her home, Verity was to discover, as she drove sedately up the drive, that she had never been more wrong.

The fact that all the lights in the house appeared to be blazing away, which they would not have been had the thrifty Trudy been in on her own, tipped Verity off that her father had not gone out as he had planned. But to find that the car Holt had once given her a lift in was parked outside told her that he, for some reason, had not yet left. Though the sight of his car was to give her no hint that it was not the lights in the house alone that were blazing!

The first intimation she had of that was when, before she had barely had time to take the keys out of the ignition, the front door was pulled back, and Holt came down the steps—fast—and yanked her, without apology, out from behind the steering wheel.

That he was blisteringly angry about something did not need two guesses. But as that hand fixed on her arm in a vicelike grip and he hauled her up the steps to the front door, for all her heart did an excited leap, he had pushed her into the hall before she had sufficient wind to drawl:

'I thought you were leaving?'

The glint that came to his furious eyes advised her to hold her tongue. But when she would have risked giving vent to her objection to being so manhandled anyway, what he came back with succeeded in making her dumb with astonishment.

'I stayed,' he said tautly, absolutely furious with her about something, she could tell, for all he was this side, just, of losing his temper completely, 'when you nearly gave your father heart failure at the way you careered down the drive nine hours ago!'

Her jaw dropping, sudden panic for her father rushing in, Verity was relieved to see her father, never in better health if his angry roar at seeing her was anything to go by, come striding from his study, where he wasted no time in laying into her.

'I've told you before about driving like a maniac!' he yelled, grabbing hold of her other arm as Holt threw from him the one he was holding. 'You've had us both worried sick!'

'Both—of you?' she exclaimed faintly, having long since forgotten the way she had sent her car hurtling over the gravel, and not quite able to reconcile in her mind Holt too being worried about her.

'Of course, both of us!' Clement Diamond bellowed, when she could hear him quite well from this close. 'Holt has spent the best part of this day looking for you!'

'He has?' she exclaimed, unable to check a glance at where Holt was stern-faced and watching her.

'Having witnessed your lunatic driving,' Holt said grimly, to let her know that he too had seen the way she had taken off, 'and with the knowledge of how that lunatic driving had you writing off a car once before, I didn't need your father to convince me that one of us should go looking for you while the other rang round the hospitals.'

'Good grief!' was all she was capable of uttering in her astonishment—it was about all she had time for, for her father was again giving forth:

'Good grief, is right!' he raged. 'Well, you can just lock that car up and throw away the key. I'm not allowing you to drive again until you've learned to control your temper!' And so angry was he with her that while Verity looked at him stunned, not believing any of it, he lost control of *his* temper, and roared, 'In fact you can give me your car keys—*now*!'

Her car keys had been dangling in her hand, but when, without waiting for her to hand them over, he snatched them out of her loose grip, it bruised her pride that he should act so, and in front of Holt.

'It was *his* fault,' she reared up angrily, sending Holt a look of dislike. It was his fault too, she fumed, remembering his mocking, 'It could be that I've fallen in love with you.'

'Heaven preserve us!' raged her father, looking thunderous that she should try to put the blame on his guest. Then, as if he'd had enough, he was striding away to his study, advising Holt as he went that he would ring round and tell everybody that she was home, and adding, 'I wash my hands of her!'

To say that she was embarrassed to be left standing in the hall with Holt Jepherson, her car keys taken from her, and having just heard her father say that he washed his hands of her, was an understatement.

'He—doesn't really mean it,' she mumbled, something needing to be said to get her over her embarrassment.

'It would serve you right if he did,' was his uncompromising answer.

'Don't *you* start!' Verity replied spiritedly.

In no mind to let him take over from where her father had left off, she walked away from him and towards the staircase. But only to find that Holt was climbing the stairs with her when, shortly, he asked:

'So where did you go when you took off as if all the devils in hell were at your heels?'

Halfway up the staircase, Verity stopped, her eyes going to his still angry expression. 'Would you believe, looking for someone more palatable than you to marry?' she asked. And refusing to be defeated that his eyes were glittering dangerously, 'You're not the only money-bags of my acquaintance, you know.'

For a dreadful second she had the idea that he was going to pitch her head-first back down the way she had just come. Though when his expression lightened, she was forewarned that his tongue might prove the sharper weapon. But she hung on to what cool he left her with when, his voice silky, he murmured:

'But you can't fancy a *full* marriage with any of the men in that crowd you run around with, can you, Verity? Or you'd certainly be minus your virginity by now.'

She shrugged—it was an effort. 'How do I know?' she asked, seemingly casually. 'I've told you that you're the only man whose bed I've been in.' She tried another shrug. 'Who's to say I don't . . .' Her careless attitude started to slip; she dragged it back. 'Who knows,' she started again, 'I might be like that with any man once—er—things start to happen.'

'I know,' said Holt, his usual overbearing confident self, she thought.

'You would!' she retorted. Though strangely, and lord knew what it was that was digging into her, but she just could not resist the question, which didn't seem to her then to be just idle curiosity, 'Er—have you been to bed with many women?' she had to ask.

The answer she received was an abrupt, 'The only thing that should concern you is how many women I go to bed with from now on.'

That he must again be referring to this marriage business gave her something of a jolt. Yet, to her surprise, it did not anger or confuse her this time. But, the oddest thing to date, instead of that anger and confusion, suddenly she was experiencing the most peculiar sensation of being lighthearted that Holt was again on that tack.

'You're saying,' she said slowly, some lighthearted wickedness all at once in charge of her, 'that you're not going to—er—um—do—er—naughties any more—until you're married?'

Odder still was the way her heart suddenly, of its own accord, started to pound when all sign of sternness left his expression and he grinned at her for her cheek. And then, as if to let her know that his marriage meant her marriage, he said clearly:

'If you have any ideas about having a long engagement—forget 'em.'

It was to save herself from grinning back like an idiot that Verity turned to face the way she had been going, and started up the rest of the stairs. But her heart pounded faster than ever when Holt, taking each stair with her, suddenly placed an arm about her shoulders.

With her heart immediately going to beat fit to burst, frantically, never ever at a loss for words before, Verity searched round for something to say.

'D-Did you really go looking for me?' she asked.

'I'm not such a bad chap really,' he replied, the smile in his voice doing nothing in the way of helping to steady her, she found. Though the smile was missing when next he spoke, and she had the sobering influence she needed, when he went on to make it plain that it was not from concern for her that he had gone searching, but his concern for her father which had motivated him, when he said, 'I thought it might be more constructive to find you and bring you home than to stay and watch Clement's mental torment as he imagined your present car to be the same mangled wreck you made of your previous one.'

'Anybody could have skidded on black ice that time,' she thought to tell him. But, chastened, as they reached the top of the stairs and Holt went along the landing with her, 'I'll make it up to him tomorrow,' she said quietly.

'I'm sure you will,' he murmured, halting with her when they reached the door of her room, and making her heart pound again that he was not biting her head off, but that he seemed for once in tune with her, as he commented quietly, 'In any event, you're home safe now.'

'Yes,' choked Verity softly, not a word of argument in her for the man she had thought she hated, but whom, she now knew, she did not.

Warm grey eyes were gently on her then, his eyes not leaving the wide-eyed look of her, when he thought to qualify that statement.

'But, if you want to stay that way, might I suggest that you don't take it into your head to go walk-about in the early hours of tomorrow morning.'

The grin which she had not wanted him to see a minute ago was beyond her control then, as she looked up at him, her lips parted in a wide smile.

'You're staying the night?'

Holt nodded, his eyes transferred to her curving mouth. 'Don't expect me to let you off a second time,' she heard him mutter. And it seemed the most natural thing in the world then, that when his head started to come down, she should reach up to receive his kiss.

As tenderly as before, he kissed her. And both his arms were about her then as he held her firmly to him. But, just as his arms had pulled her yet closer and his kiss had deepened, so, as he began to trigger off wild emotions in her, Holt gently pushed her from him.

Aware that she had not put up so much as an atom of resistance, Verity was stilent when his gaze went from her bemused face, and he opened the door of her room.

'Goodnight, Verity,' he said firmly then, and had pushed her inside her room, and the door was closed— with Holt on the other side of it.

'Goodnight, Holt,' whispered Verity, as in a dream she crossed to her bed. 'Goodnight, my darling,' she breathed, and knew it was not hate she felt for him, but love.

With such a tenderness surging in her for him, Verity went and sat on the edge of her bed. I love him, she thought, and it just did not seem right that she should be there in her room without him.

For a long time she sat just thinking and thinking about the man who, when everything was against it, had walked in and stolen her heart. And when eventually she automatically went into the bathroom to wash and to get into her night things, then got into bed, her thoughts were still with him.

Wide awake, though with a dreamy expression on her face, she had not the remotest chance of going to sleep. Especially she could not sleep when, with excitement drumming in her, she found she was in the desperate state of wanting to know how Holt felt about her.

Proof that he had desired her lay in the way in which he had firmly pushed her into her room, just as though the temptation of letting his kiss get out of hand was nearly too much for him.

A smile peeped out as again and again she relieved his 'Don't expect me to let you off a second time'. Oh, Holt, my darling, my love, she thought, and she willed him to come for her. But he did not.

Holt was Verity's first thought, as he had been her last, when she awoke the next morning. But the dreams which she had woven last night, where maybe Holt felt just a fraction of the love for her which she felt for him, did not, with the coming of daylight, seem to have any semblance of the reality they'd had then.

It was then that agitation started to attack her nervous system. Unable to stay in bed a moment longer, she went to shower and to dress with her mind taken up with wondering about his stated intention that he would marry her.

She emerged from the bathroom still anxious, and holding her breath at thinking that, what with him being a man of his word and everything, dared she let herself believe that for him to consider using that escape clause—which meant he would be backing out of his agreement with her father—Holt must want to marry her pretty badly?

She knew, of course, that Holt was not in love with her. But, since he must like her a little to have kissed her at all last night, then surely, if she was married to him, would she not be in a first-class position to get him to fall in love with her?

The decision was already made that, not wanting a long engagement either, she would marry him at the first opportunity; suddenly, desperately wanting to see him, Verity shot from her room.

She was halfway down the stairs before she wished she had thought to wear something more sophisticated than the jeans and sweater she had put on. But her longing to see him made her disobey the impulse to go back and change. And in no time, she was tripping across the hall and pausing in a useless effort to find some sort of composure, then she was entering the breakfast room.

To find her parent sitting in his usual place, but no sign at all of Holt, was something of a let-down. But excitement at the thought that any minute now he would be joining them had her not recognising that her father had no returning smile to offer her.

'Good morning, Papa,' she bade him cheerfully, because it wasn't his fault that he wasn't Holt. 'Is something the matter?' she asked when instead of answering her, he favoured her with a grim look.

'*Good God!*' he roared suddenly to make her jump. 'Don't tell me you've *forgotten*?'

'Oh, Dad, I'm sorry,' said Verity in genuine regret, not wondering that it had gone from her completely that her parent had been as mad as hell with her last night, and that she didn't deserve to be let off lightly this morning.

'So you damn well should be!' he exploded. 'When I think of . . .'

'I won't ever go off like that again,' she butted in at the gallop—if she was to be hauled over the coals then she wanted it over with before Holt came down.

'You're damn right about that!' she was told forthrightly. 'While I have any say in the matter, you won't be driving yourself *anywhere*!'

Verity could not hold back on the smile that started in her at the implication she saw behind his words. It was quite obvious to her, then, that with him saying, 'While I have any say in the matter,' the dear love was getting ready to let go his hold on the reins.

But, 'You can smile,' he was telling her heavily before she could make any reply. 'But you'll be smiling on the other . . .'

'Don't be a crosspatch, darling,' she interrupted softly, going on quickly when he turned a tinge apoplectic, 'I know you have every right to be angry with me, but . . .' her smile became self-conscious as she confessed, '. . . but the—circumstances of yesterday were—rather exceptional, weren't they?'

'You're not joking—they *were* exceptional,' he retorted sharply, in no way mollified. '*Never* did I expect to hear what I heard in my study yesterday morning!'

'I didn't mean that,' Verity said hurriedly, vividly remembering his embarrassment of the previous morning. She recalled then how he had said he was trying his hardest to be modern-minded, and she guessed he had been stunned, when like most fathers he still thought of his daughter as his little girl, to learn that she had been in Holt's bed, and he had been made to realise how fully a woman she was. Hastily she went on, 'Though it does have some bearing on what we discussed yesterday.'

'What, exactly, *did* you mean?' asked Clement Diamond, angrily perplexed. And with a suddenly appalled start, 'The saints preserve us!' he exclaimed. 'Don't tell me there's more!' His bushy eyebrows came down then, and his voice was stern, when he threatened furiously, 'If you've been up to any . . .'

'I haven't. Honestly, I haven't,' Verity rushed to tell him. And because there was such a tremendous excitement burning in her, and because she wanted him as happy as she was and not glowering at her the way he was, she told him what she knew would please him—for hadn't she seen keenness in him yesterday at his thoughts of her marrying Holt? 'You know what it is anyway,' she said, and her smile peeping out again, 'You knew before I did.'

His exasperated look told her that he had not got around yet to remembering how he had told her, even if he had got it slightly wrong about it being love at first sight, that he knew she was in love with Holt. But, as if he still suspected she was up to mischief, there was no smile there to relieve his stern expression, as he said sharply:

'I'm not into guessing games, Verity.'

'You were yesterday,' she replied with a grin. But there was a tender look in her eyes, as she said softly, 'You guessed then, and you were right, that I was in love with Holt.'

Never had she thought to make her father speechless. But as Clement Diamond looked at the dreamy gentle look in her eyes, his face took on the expression of a man who was positively staggered. And it was to take several moments before he had recovered sufficient of his equilibrium to ask:

'Are you—serious?'

'Never more so,' she replied, her smile starting to waver at his shaken look.

'This isn't just—another of your far-fetched ideas to put me off the . . .'

'Far-fetched?' she queried, her puzzlement added to the fact that he looked visibly troubled. But she was at pains then to let him see that he need never trouble his head about her again. 'I know that I must have shocked you dreadfully with some of my—er—capers,' she said. 'But I can promise you that that's all in the past.' Her smile returned then, because to hear that from now on he was to have a model daughter seemed to have winded him. And her voice had taken on that tender, gentle tone again, when softly she told him, 'I've fallen in love with Holt, Dad,' and a little helplessly, her hands spread in a small movement, she went on, 'Don't ask me how it happened, because I've no idea. But what I do know is that, loving him so much, all I want is to marry him and . . .'

She would have gone on. There was so much emotion in this all-consuming love that had grown in her without her ever being aware of it. But the pain in her father's voice as he cut her off, as though he couldn't bear to hear any more, stopped her. And it was her turn to look staggered, and disbelieving, when, with so much anguish in him, he said:

'Holt is not going to marry you.'

They had shared a joke before, she and her father. Sometimes, when the mood was on him, he would tease her outrageously. But as Verity stared at the deadly serious expression he wore, she knew that this was no joke, and he was not teasing her out of devilment. But still something in her would not let her believe what he had just said.

'You're—wrong,' she denied, her voice cracking to see that there was no change in that expression to tell her that the joke was over, that his teasing was at an end. 'H-Holt told me himself that he would marry me. He . . .'

Clement Diamond shaking his head made her break off. But he seemed unable to watch and see that hope in her fade, and in a rush to get it over with as quickly as possible, he said:

'Holt wasn't serious. He just told you what he and I, between us, agreed he would tell you.'

'You—agreed . . .' her voice faded, and with the colour draining away from her face, she heard her father quickly confessing his part in how he and Holt had set her up!

'To save me the embarrassment of Mrs Trueman telling me what she found when she went into his room yesterday morning, Holt told me the truth of how you came to be in his bed. He . . .'

'He told you the truth!' Verity gasped almost inaudibly. 'He told you how I planned to—to trick him by . . .'

Clement Diamond nodded, and admitted, 'Not to put too fine a point on it, and regardless of the tact

Holt displayed in the telling, I was never more embarrassed in my life. Mortified and furious, I felt I could happily have wrung your neck for the intolerable position you'd put me in.'

A kind of numbness had set in Verity. She felt dead inside and unable to even feel contrition that her father should, through her, be made to feel so dreadful.

'You—told Holt—how you felt?' she asked jerkily.

'I didn't need to,' he replied. 'He could see how I felt before I exploded that by God, you were going to be made to pay for this.'

'And Holt—he saw a very good way to make me pay, didn't he?' she asked, glad of that numbness, never wanting that numbness to leave, because when it did, she knew that the pain, the unbearable pain, would start. 'It was *his* idea, wasn't it?' she asked, but had no real need to hear her father's reply.

'I was blowing my top about you,' her father owned. 'But when I said that I'd see to it your future freedom was curtailed, even if I had to lock you in your room at night—a bit excessive, I admit,' he inserted, 'but I was in a boiling rage with you at the time—well, Holt suggested that if I wanted to give you something else to think about, you'd get the shock of your life if you thought the result of your own actions was that you would have to marry him.'

'You thought it a good idea?' Verity asked tonelessly.

'I did up until the time I found myself telling you about the financial difficulties the firm had been in. Any anger in me was then for myself, that I hadn't had the courage to ignore my pride and tell you the true reason why I had to break my promise to you. But,' he went on, 'when in next to no time I saw that not only had you bounced back but that you were driving like a bat out of hell down the drive, I was again so furious with you that I vowed then and there that if you survived your reckless driving in one piece, if Holt's plan gave you the fright of your life, then you deserved it, because it was nothing to the fright you'd given me!'

The shock of what she had heard was starting to recede. The pain was starting to bite. But Verity had pride too—an abundance of it.

'Guess who slid on the banana skin,' she said airily. But as a brave attempt at a joke, it didn't come off. For the huskiness in her voice, and the way, without her knowing it, her hands were clenched as she fought to stay on top of her emotions until she could get to somewhere private, gave her away.

'I'm so sorry, darling,' said Clement Diamond sadly, fully aware of the same pride in him which had been passed down to his daughter. And forgetful of his trust in the other man, suddenly, a degree sharply, he asked, 'Holt never gave you any reason to suppose he was in love with you—did he?'

She shook her head. No, Holt had not done that. Nor would he ever. Only now could she see how with that feeling of love for him burning in her, she had blithely thought that any liking he had for her—that liking no more than wishful thinking on her part, she saw now—could be turned into love.

'No,' she said, and, never one to show her tears, determined not to break down in front of her father, 'he never once mentioned the word love. He just implied that if—that if I didn't agree to marry him, he would use some escape clause to get out of the contract he has with you, and that—that would leave you back to worrying, and the firm ruined.'

Given that what she had just said had come out sounding a little fractured, Verity had managed to live through what Holt had told her without tears. But if her tears were held back, the same could not be said for her open-mouthed astonishment, when her father told her quietly:

'There is no such escape clause, Verity.'

'No such . . .!'

'I'm sorry, truly sorry,' he said, 'but . . .' Helplessly he shook his head. 'But in fairness,' he continued, 'and in the face of the enormity of what you did, and were still prepared to do to blacken Holt's character had he not been up to you, it didn't at the time seem to be such a very great sin to use any means to . . .' He broke off, like her hearing someone coming.

Holt! she thought, and she was on her feet, not yet ready to face him, her eyes looking feverishly for somewhere to hide.

'It's only Mrs Trueman,' said her father, putting the correct construction on the way she looked set for flight.

'He'll be here in a moment,' she said urgently, still ready to be off.

'Holt has already left.'

'He's—gone!'

'He has a business appointment up north at nine,' he said, adding when Verity still looked ready to flee and as though she didn't believe that Holt had a nine o'clock business appointment anywhere on a Sunday morning, 'He's meeting his architects on some building site where he's considering building a factory.'

Conversation was temporarily halted when Mrs Trueman, looking no sweeter than she had looked yesterday, came in with coffee and toast for Verity, and then, without a word, went out again.

But Trudy in a mood had little effect on Verity that morning. And having no interest in coffee, or toast either, she thought there was little more her father could have to tell her. Though before she left the breakfast room, there was one very urgent promise which she had to have from him.

'Dad,' she said, getting his attention before she said his name, 'I know that—before—force of circumstances left you with no alternative but to break your word to me. But may I have your promise now that, whatever the circumstances, Holt Jepherson will never know from you about my—my love for him?'

'As if I'd . . .' Clement Diamond began to protest.

'Promise,' Verity insisted, her pride demanding that Holt never knew the extent of just how foolish she had been.

She was aware she was tense just as she was aware of her father's eyes on her tense expression. But, at last, he gave her that promise she so needed.

'You have my word on it, love,' he said, 'my unbreakable word, that regardless of any and all circumstances, Holt shall never know of our conversation this morning.'

CHAPTER NINE

HAD there been only herself to consider, Verity would have spent that Sunday when her hopes were being split asunder with no company but her own. But, with the hurt in her like a raw bleeding wound, for her father's sake she went down to eat a lunch she did not want.

But catching his worried eyes on her from time to time, she was reminded of the other burden of worry that had so recently been his. It was his anxiety for her that decided her against returning to the privacy of her room.

'So,' she said brightly, 'how about letting me in on all this ruffing and finessing I hear about?'

'You want to learn about Bridge?' he asked, his expression lightening.

'Well,' she hedged, aware that it took years to learn the finer points of the game, 'perhaps not all, but I'm at your disposal for a few hours.' Which brought on the prompt enquiry:

'You're going out tonight?'

About to say no, though she had a vague recollection that the gang were meeting up at the Dog and Trumpet later, Verity suddenly knew from those anxious looks that if she did, he would be cancelling any arrangements he had for the evening in order to keep her company.

'I'm supposed to be seeing Miranda and a few of the others later,' she said, aware he had missed out on his Bridge party last night through her. 'But I'll stay in if . . .'

'No, no,' he refused to hear of it, not deceiving her for a second that he thought it would take her mind off Holt to be out with her friends. 'I half promised I'd make up a four at the Risdales',' he explained.

She bade her father a cheerful farewell when at half past seven he went out. And, not wanting Miranda, or anyone else, to phone or call round when she didn't show up at the Dog and Trumpet, she adopted the same cheerful attitude when she rang her friend to invent a tummy bug.

But when the phone went down, down too went her cheerful exterior, and for the next few hours the fight that had always been intrinsic in her spirited personality deserted her. She felt utterly defeated, and could not even wish to have back the hate she had thought she had felt for Holt. She loved him, and that meant that despite him outsmarting her in the way he had, she still could not hate him.

It was a little after ten when Verity thought she might just as well get into bed and wonder how other people coped who gave their love where it was not wanted, as to stay in her chair and ponder if the day would ever come when she did not feel so thoroughly dejected, when the phone in her room rang.

Knowing that Trudy would assume it was for her, Verity crossed to her bedside table and picked up the receiver. But when, forcing a lightness into her tones, she gave her number, she very nearly dropped to hear the voice of none other than—Holt Jepherson!

Her nerves an instant agitated jumble, she had said a speedy, 'My father isn't in,' before she could think. But she was to be shaken into realising that, of course, Holt had no idea that his insincere proposal to marry her had been rumbled when, his manner easy, he replied:

'Is that an invitation for me to come over?' It was

then that something inside her started to snap. And it was still in the process of snapping, when, as she had not answered, Holt went on, 'It wasn't your father I wanted to speak to.'

My God! she thought. But with the fight in her still struggling to give the pain in her a hiding, what she had meant to come out as sarcastic did not sound at all sarcastic to her ears, but to her mind she sounded quite docile when she offered:

'You were aching for the sound of your fiancée's voice?'

There was a slight pause from the other end. But she was made aware that the sarcasm she had meant had just not come off when, with a trace of seduction, she would swear, that pause ended with Holt saying:

'Come to think of it, Verity, you do have rather a pleasing quality to your voice.'

Not about to risk sarcasm a second time only for it not to come off, but aware of a renewal of life in her, Verity fought hard to keep her voice even when she thought to ask, 'Er—was there any special reason for your call?' but only to have the adrenalin of anger surge through her veins, when he said:

'I was hoping to call in person, but I got delayed. I rang to make arrangements to take you to dinner tomorrow.'

That there seemed no end to his nerve sent her mercury soaring ever higher. But she was taking no chances on saying too much if she once let fly.

Though from where she got the control to be able to tell him evenly, 'Actually, Holt, I've made other arrangements for tomorrow evening,' she never knew.

But that small control she had won was to go rocketing from her in an explosion of fury, as she heard the edge of anger in his tone, his aggression on the warpath, when, his voice no longer easy, he said sharply:

'You *are* aware that we're to be married?'

'I'm as aware of it as you are!' she hurled straight back. In the next second she had crashed the phone down.

Mutiny was still high in her half an hour later. She was still gasping at his colossal impudence as she paced her bedroom floor. Heavens, she fumed, that he should *dare* to pretend to object that she had a date with someone else!

When Verity finally went to bed, she was to sleep only fitfully. And each time she awoke, she would seethe that, by the look of it, Holt Jepherson was ready to continue to play the prospective bridegroom until presumably such time as he would take great delight in telling her that no one tried to pull a fast one on him without paying for it.

She finally awakened to find that it was no longer dark outside. But that morning she was to discover that the fight in her was still alive and well, in that her first thought was: so Holt Jepherson thought he would string her along until the time came for him to tell her, 'Don't tangle with me unless you want another lesson in one-upmanship,' did he?

Though her fingers had been severely burnt the last time, Verity went over and over again every angle of what she was going to do to steal *his* thunder this time. Oh, wouldn't it be just what he deserved that when he charmingly told her that not only did he not consider himself engaged to her, but that he had never, from the very beginning, had any intention of marrying her, to be able to smile sweetly, her pride fully restored, and say a careless, 'Oh, I know that—what else is new?'

She went once again over everything in her mind, and then, her spirit refusing point blank to lie down, she thought, why the hell not? If Holt wanted to play games, who was she to spoil his fun?

It was a bright Verity who joined her father at breakfast that morning. And if he looked a little quizzical that, before he returned her car keys to her, all seemed very much better with her world this morning, then Verity was pleased. One thing had been achieved at any rate; he had gone to his office looking much less anxious about her than he had looked yesterday.

She left it until she thought Holt would have settled into his office for the day before she took her first steps to put her plan of campaign into action. Then, a frequent visitor to her father's study, she had no difficulty in finding his list of prime telephone numbers. As she had suspected, Holt's number was there.

The mention that she was Clement Diamond's daughter showed her how much respect her father's name had in Holt's office, in that in no time Holt's secretary was putting her through to him.

But, feeling her way, she had no thought of backing down, even when to hear his voice had her gritting her teeth at the weakness that assaulted her.

'I'm sorry I put the phone down on you last night,' she began, in what she hoped was a suitably contrite voice. 'You rather caught me on the hop.' And rushing on in case he returned the compliment and slammed the phone down on her, though why he should she couldn't imagine, for the game, as he thought, was all his, 'I'm ringing to ask if you were serious about taking me to dinner?'

The reply she received was swift, sarcastic, and guaranteed to make her want to thump him.

'Your date has stood you up?'

Telling herself that she couldn't allow herself the privilege of losing her temper at the first hurdle, Verity hung grimly in there, and seized at the opening he had given her.

'It's not a date so much as a last meeting with Jolyon Robey,' she said quietly. But, having to go on when no help was coming from the other end, she further perjured her soul by saying, 'I thought, in the circumstances, that I ought to tell him I won't be seeing him again.'

Dead silence at the other end made her resist the temptation to again treat Holt to her crashing-the-phone-down-in-his-ear technique. But at last, sounding nothing like the lover he was supposed to be, his voice came, shortly, down the wires.

'You're that close that you can't give Robey his marching orders over the phone?'

'He *has* asked me to marry him,' Verity thought to point out. And not wanting a discussion on Jolyon Robey, but too hurt to care how many lies she told, 'You can't read my mind, I know,' she went on, 'but I thought, last night when you rang, that you too might need a free evening in which to—to—er . . .'

'To clear away any dead wood from my past?'

'Something like that,' she agreed, and had a dent knocked in her determination in that her heart gave a definite uplift, when he said:

'There's no one *that* close.' But his voice had grown warmer when he asked, 'Are you going to put the phone down on me if I suggest I should like to take you out tomorrow night?'

Verity came away from the phone with her eyes shining because she had a date with Holt for tomorrow. But that was until she remembered that this was no ordinary date. All too soon then reality was rushing in, and she was rapidly smoothing out that dent which he had made in her determination. In all probability, she thought, Holt planned to give up not a thing, but would be two-timing her with Selene Aston all the way along.

She had plenty of time during that Monday in which to stiffen her resolve, though she allowed some time out of that day to phone around a few friends to intimate that she was going away for a short holiday, and would ring again when she was back in circulation. That done, there was only her father to deceive. And much though she disliked having to deceive him at all, since he was certain to bump into Holt if it was more than one date she was to have with him, then deceive him she would have to.

'You're going out with Holt tomorrow evening!' he exclaimed in astonishment when, with not so much as a hint of the hurt digging away at her, she had told him, making believe it had been today, not last night, how Holt had telephoned.

'I know nothing will come of my seeing him, Dad,' said Verity, and she was sadly sincere about that, 'but,' she smiled brightly, 'just in case he's somehow picked up how I feel about him, I thought that maybe to accept his invitation would give me a chance to show him differently.'

Her father's steady probing look made her fearful for a second or two that he was suspicious that she might be plotting something. But her fears were proved groundless, when after another look to the tilt of her chin, all he had to say was an admiring:

'The Diamond pride, eh!'

Verity was to witness admiration of a different sort, and in another man's eyes, the following evening when Holt came to call for her.

'My father is putting in a late stint at the office,' she excused his absence.

'May I be forgiven for being glad it's the daughter I've called for and not the father,' said Holt gallantly, his eyes taking in the shine of her newly washed hair, her flawless light make-up, and the figure-hugging jersey dress she had deliberated on so long before she had decided that none other would do.

Her racing heart betraying her, she smiled a natural smile and turned from him, seeking control, as she said, 'I'll just get my bag.'

In the car, sitting this close to the dinner-jacketed, broad-shouldered man who thought he was taking her for a ride, Verity had again to fight against the thrill of just being with him. She thought she had just about made it, when Holt enquired:

'You've set your house in order, Verity?'

'House?' she asked, wondering if everyone discovered they had cotton wool for a brain when they fell in love.

'Have you told Robey that you're—otherwise engaged?'

'Oh yes,' she lied, and for authenticity's sake, 'He—er—wasn't very pleased about it, I'm afraid.'

'Tough,' was all the sympathy he had.

The restaurant Holt took her to was one she had not been to before. Though with the romantically subdued lighting, there was little chance of her getting a good look around. But, determined as she was to play her part well, she was soon to find that the magnetism which Holt had for her was making it all uphill work to remember that it was only a part she was playing.

All too easily he had her laughing at any of the amusing quips he made, and countless were the times, as they ate their way through each delicious course, when he was to have her lips parting in a smile.

But her smile, her mouth, seemed to have some interest for him in that when his eyes were not on her eyes, they would stray to her lips. It must, she thought, all be part of this light seduction he was practising on her senses.

But alarm bells suddenly jangled when having finished the last course and in the middle of coffee, Holt, his eyes again on her eyes, said casually:

'Would you mind if we called in at my place before I take you home?'

Would she ever! Not content with leading her up the garden path, she saw he was planning to round the evening off by going the whole hog by having a cosy little seduction scene up his sleeve for when they reached his home!

'It won't take a moment,' he added, a world of persuasive charm in his smile.

Like hell it wouldn't, Verity thought. But, just when right then she might very well have blown it, winging in came the memory of how she had determined to play along with him right up to the moment when he revealed he had not the slightest intention of marrying her.

'Do you want to go now?' she asked, her eyes wide and innocent, hiding totally the thought that since the success of what *she* had planned meant she would have to go along some of the way to meet him, that didn't mean that she wasn't going to hit him if he had any subtle suggestion to make such as 'Would you like to see the décor of my bedroom?'

Of the opinion, from the speed with which Holt drove to Drake's Knighton, that he would be making a grab for her before he'd got the front door closed, Verity had to think again when he did no more than touch her elbow as he guided her into his drawing room.

But she wasn't fooled for a moment when, with a glance at his watch, Holt moved away from her to go to a small and elegant desk, saying over his shoulder as he went, 'Part of the reason why I wanted to call in here was so you could have a look round your future home.'

How sweet, she thought sourly, not needing an explanation for the other part of his reason. Naturally, any tour of his home would just have to include a look round the upstairs part of the house, wouldn't it?

Not knowing why she should feel so disappointed in him that he should prove such a smooth operator, for she had had no illusions about him before he had called for her, she had a valiant smile on her face when, collecting something from the desk drawer, he returned to stand close up to her. But wary of him, watching for his next move, she was puzzled when with his eyes fixed on hers, he said quietly:

'Since we have an hour's run to Lower Bassett, I'll show you over the rest of the rooms another time.'

'Oh,' escaped her in surprise. But it was quickly followed by, 'Perhaps it is a little late,' as she wondered how long was this charade going to go on.

'The other part of my reason for bringing you here,' Holt went on, while Verity waited, hoping she could handle it without giving in to the need to punch his head, 'was because I wasn't sure that your father might not still be up when I took you home.'

She guessed then that this was all part of his seduction technique, and she could not deny that she felt disappointment again at his less than subtle hint that he didn't want her father around when he went into action.

'My father does sometimes work very late in his study,' she murmured.

'I imagined as much,' said Holt, in confirmation of her suspicions. Though he was to throw her completely when, his hand coming up to show her the small square box he held, he told her, 'I wanted to be private when I gave you—this.'

All thought and all speech went from Verity then as, utterly stunned, she saw him pull back the lid to expose the most exquisite diamond solitaire ring.

She was still staring witlessly, when Holt took hold of her left hand and slid the solitaire over her engagement finger.

'Do you like it?' he asked, when not so much as a peep had come from her.

'Oh, Holt!' she cried, and she was so taken aback that when he leaned forward and placed a tender kiss on her cheek, there was not so much as one single thought in her head that 'whole hog' did not begin to cover the lengths he was going to, in order to play out this charade.

Tears of emotion were welling up inside her, as, unable to say anything more, she took her eyes from her ring and looked at the man who had somehow now got his arm around her. And, 'Oh, Holt,' she said again. It seemed out of the question then that they should not kiss.

And once his mouth was over hers, Verity had no chance of remembering any of how she had planned to have the last laugh. For her emotions had been attacked before he had taken her in his arms, and once she was in his arms, she knew nothing but that in his arms was where she wanted to be.

There was no chance then either, as she clung to him and gave him kiss for kiss, that it would stop at just a few kisses. For soon she was on fire for him, hungry for him, and wanting more and yet more as he aroused that same need for her that he had aroused in her before.

And as Holt's mouth plundered hers, and his lips sought the hollows in her throat, Verity was pliant in his arms. She had no idea when his jacket had been removed, or when the zip of her dress had been lowered; or indeed whether he had carried her to the couch, or if she had walked there. But it was sheer bliss to have his hands caressing her as they pressed closer and closer together.

The pink hardened peaks of her breasts were throbbing out her need under his hands. Hands which roved and caressed from her breasts to the satin skin of her belly, drawing from her a gasp, a sigh, and a moan of wanting as his hands caressed back and he cupped her face, and again he kissed her. Passion was riding him too, as he took her past the point where their lovemaking had ceased before.

But Verity was not thinking of that other time when Holt had made a nonsense of her thinking. Nor did she need to remember it. That was until, his eyes blazing with the fierce flame of his need for her, Holt groaned, 'Oh God—how I want you!' And again assaulting her senses, he continued to kiss her while his hands seemed incapable of resisting the temptation to fondle the swollen naked globes of her breasts. 'I had to let you go before,' he murmured, 'but not now—you're mine.'

Her tender smile of full agreement was halfway there, then all at once, not needed, and definitely not wanted, the memory came screaming into her head of Holt saying—when inwardly he must have been laughing his head off—'Don't expect me to let you off a second time'.

On that instant, still not thinking coherently, but acting more on instinct, Verity was galvanised into jet-propelled action. And having shot from the couch, she was standing rocking where she stood, in shock, instinct again her aid as she tried to make sense of what appeared to be a bra with ten shoulder straps since she couldn't find the right ones to get her arms through.

'What the . . .' Holt was standing too. But Verity was not looking at him.

'I—can't,' she said jerkily, and found that her hands had been knocked away from what she had been trying to achieve by way of getting some clothing about her, and that Holt, the flush of desire still on his face, had gripped her by her arms and had swung her round to face him.

'You *can't*!' His expression was incredulous as his eyebrows went up. 'My God, you were . . .'

'I know what I was, and . . . and I know what I am,' cried Verity shakily, and it was touch and go then that the whole of it would not come tumbling out from her lips.

'You want me, damn you,' he grated harshly, and would have taken her back in his arms then, had she let him. But, visibly trembling, she pulled fiercely out of his hold, his touch on her of no help in her need to get herself together again, and fast.

'Of—of course I want you,' she cried, her voice rising hysterically, tears stinging her eyes at knowing that it was not just physically that she wanted him, and the agony of knowing that they would never be as one.

Wanting to run away, to hide, to hide her hurt, and to never come out of hiding, Verity did not know how much of his arguing she could take.

But, whether it was from hearing her admission that she wanted him, though she thought she had left him with very little doubt about that, or whether he had seen the battle she was putting up not to let her tears fall, she did not know. But it was not his arguing she was to be faced with, for with his tone much less aggressive, Holt left argument, and went to look for reasons.

'Can you tell me what went wrong?' he asked, a controlled kind of quietness in his voice.

She saw his glance flick to where the tips of her breasts were still the hard peaks he had made of them, and she was hastily then trying to do something about covering herself up.

'N-nothing w-went wrong,' she stammered, her voice coming out so wobbly that Holt had moved to assist her, more able than she to make two bra straps out of the ten she had found.

'You're shaking like a leaf,' he muttered as, her dress back over her shoulders, he zipped her up.

But feeling a shade more normal to be looking more or less the way she had when she had arrived at his home, so as the aggressive thought came that it was no one's fault but his that she was 'shaking like a leaf', Verity started to think in more orderly patterns. Though she had to own that it was something of a relief when Holt took his hands from her, even though, continuing to probe, he came round to face her.

'Something must have happened for you to bolt from me like that,' he said, but as he said it, all at once all his aggression departed, and there was a definite softening in him when, with a thread of understanding, he asked, 'Did you suddenly get scared?' and with more understanding, 'There was no need to panic, I wouldn't have rushed you. I . . .'

'It wasn't that,' her honesty had her quickly confessing before she was able to get herself together, to invent, 'We—you and I—w-we're not married yet.'

'Good God!' he exclaimed, just as though that was the last thing he had expected to hear. And that made her mad!

'It's all right for you!' she flared hotly. 'But it's me who has to go home and face my father.'

'You think he doesn't know that—this sort of thing—goes on?'

His sarcasm gave an extra charge to her batteries. But when she would have come firing back at him, she was to remember the honesty of her tongue of a minute before, and she was alert to danger should her tongue again become unwary.

She turned from him, needing all the control she could muster. 'You've done *this sort of thing* before,' she told him. 'I—never have.' And with that honesty catching up with her anyway, it was the truth when she confessed, 'And I—I just don't think I could look my father in the eye, when I get home.'

For an age it seemed that Holt had nothing to reply. And then, still turned from him, Verity heard him move. She was aware that his movement had been towards her, but the next thing she knew was that he had placed a light arm about her shoulders, and while her insides began to jitter again, he did no more than lead her to the door, pausing only to pick up her bag on the way.

And only at the front door did he come to a halt, and it was there that he turned her to face him, and asked softly:

'Are you going to forgive me for being so intent on possessing you that I paid no heed to the honesty which, regardless of the devilment you've got up to in the past, runs right through you?'

Too well aware of how insincere he was, she was not taken in by the sincerity of his look. But when it came to forgiving him, not least for the way he had so nearly made her his while it meant nothing to him, Verity returned his sincere look, and served him with some more of her *honesty*.

'There's nothing to forgive,' she lied smilingly. But she could have pushed him head first down the steps when, locking the front door behind them, he lingered to murmur:

'I think the sooner we have the arrangements made for our wedding, the better, don't you?'

CHAPTER TEN

IN a pensive mood, Verity sat in the drawing room at Birchwood House with her thoughts, as they were most of the time, centred on Holt Jepherson. And again she wished that the stubborn streak in her would let go so that she could be the one to end their phoney engagement. The waiting for him to be the one to put an end to it was, she owned, getting to her.

She was still wondering, as she had every day since he had put that diamond on her finger, if her next date with him would be the one where he would ask, with a few well-chosen words, for the return of his ring. It was a fact that she was fast losing sight of the few well-chosen words of her own that she had been reserving especially for that occasion.

She had been engaged to him for a month now, and contrary to her expectation that maybe within a couple of dates Holt would be making his *adieu* speech, he still hadn't said anything! And she had to admit that she didn't know which was the worst, the waiting, or the fact that when she knew full well that he thought he was taking her for a 'Ta-ta', she was more deeply in love with him now than she had been at the start.

It wasn't as if she hadn't tried to get out of the mess he made of her emotions. But although she gave herself the severest lectures on how she was not going to enjoy herself, and told herself how he must be laughing himself crazy at the way he thought he was leading her on, each outing ended the same way—with her going up to her room with stars shining in her eyes, and with the knowledge of how difficult, not to say impossible she had found it not to laugh at anything amusing he said, and how she had been in total sympathy with him on most of the subjects that had come up for discussion.

None of it, she thought despondently, made sense any more. Even her father, when she'd been a bundle of nerves about telling him her news, had been overjoyed at her engagement.

Holt would have come in with her that night when, with time going on, he had driven her home from Drake's Knighton, but she had used the lateness of the hour as an excuse for not inviting him in. Though her father had not been in bed, but trying to hide the fact that his concern for her had been his reason for staying up, he had come out of his study to ask how her date had gone, and with an attempt at lightness, to ask if Holt now had the idea that one date with him was, as far as she was concerned, just one too many.

'Not quite,' she had replied, with that damnable shine still in her eyes because although Holt had let her go after just one kiss, there had been nothing lacking in the kiss of parting he had bestowed on her. 'Actually,' she said, knowing that this was going to be the biggest lie she would ever tell him, 'I discovered that Holt feels about me exactly the same way I feel about him.'

'You mean—he's—told you he loves you?' Clement Diamond had exclaimed.

Verity could still see his look of disbelief now. That look that had changed into one that said he thought that Holt was carrying the joke too far. But that had been before she had shown him her left hand with the expensive sparkling diamond winking on her engagement finger. And although he had looked initially to be stupefied, suddenly his expression had altered.

'You're engaged to Holt!' A smile had spread across

his face then, and as he sometimes did, he was referring to his memory of his dead wife, though with a father's pride for his daughter, as he said, 'Your mother was right when she said that one day those big brown eyes of yours would bowl some man over before he knew what had hit him.'

Verity had not known quite what to expect. But that her father should so readily accept what she had just told him—when he had been in the thick of the plot which Holt had hatched—made her feel that she was the one to be the more surprised.

'You—er—don't think it's—a bit sudden?' she thought to ask.

'It happened for your mother and me that way,' he replied, his memories of that time happy memories. But as if sensing her uncertainty, he was swift to say, 'Holt has a reputation for going and getting what he's after without any messing about. But if that other business is worrying you, then with his ring on your finger, you needn't have the smallest doubt that it's you he wants.'

'It's not worrying me,' she had smiled. But she was aware then that her father did not know the new member of his board anywhere near as well as he thought he did if he believed that Holt had given up on his plans to make her squirm.

Clement Diamond had smiled too. 'Good,' he had replied, and with conviction, he had told her, 'Holt would never have given you an engagement ring had he any intention other than to marry you.'

That her father would be happy to welcome Holt as a son-in-law was obvious. And he was not the only one who was pleased at the news. For Trudy was now back to asking her if she was going to have just toast for breakfast, and had even been a little moist-eyed when she'd said she would miss her when she married and went to live at Drake's Knighton.

Miranda was another one who had surprised her by sounding dewy-eyed. Expecting that Holt would be saying his piece at any moment, Verity had let a week go by when, because she didn't know for how long she was going to have to keep on thinking up excuses for not going out with the crowd, she telephoned Miranda and told her that she was engaged to Holt.

'My giddy aunt!' squealed Miranda at first. 'I know I suggested that you should make a play for him, Verity, but I never expected you to go overboard!'

'Neither did I,' replied Verity without thinking—though overboard was a pale description for the header she had taken. She had been sinking without knowing it from the moment she had first clapped eyes on him, and she had been drowning ever since.

'Oh, Verity,' said Miranda, her voice changing to be gentle, with a touch of awe, 'it's really love, then?'

Verity coughed, but realising that she must have given herself away, she found that pride, even to her close friend, would not have her confiding all the ins and outs of everything. But Miranda was taking her silence for shyness in telling her of the truth of her feelings, and had gone on to ask:

'When's the wedding to be?'

Verity remembered how Holt had said that the sooner the arrangements for their wedding were made, the better, though the proof of how much faith she could put in that statement lay in the fact that he had made no mention of it since.

'Er—we haven't decided on a date yet,' she replied.

She spent several more minutes in talking to Miranda, but when she had come away from the phone, it was to come home to her that when Miranda had told her what she and the gang had been up to this past week, none of their escapades had seemed at all as hysterically funny as at one time she would have thought them to be. For a moment or two she had wondered if in loving Holt, she had lost her sense of humour. But she was then to recall those occasions when, forgetting everything but just being with him, effortlessly he would have the laughter bubbling up inside her.

It was then she knew that without her being aware of it, and painful though the process had been, painful though it still was, she had grown up.

But leaving the drawing room, Verity reflected that if falling in love had been the cause of her growing up, then knowing Holt had done her no favours. For when he went from her life she would not even have her friends, for having grown away from them, there would be no going back.

Verity had still not surfaced from the depression that had descended on her when she got ready to go out with Holt that night. Would it be tonight, she wondered, that he would say goodbye?

But, on edge as she had been all day, she began to be afraid that if tonight saw Holt departing with nothing having been said, then the brick wall of stubbornness that had supported her for so long might, along with her pride, go crumbling; and that she would be the one to finish what he had started. But she couldn't have that. The first move had to come from him—it just *had to*.

Though aware that she could not go on like this, just waiting for him to say that her outings with him were over—and lord knew how she was going to cope with not seeing him again—Verity was suddenly to see that if he did not make the first move soon, then she was just going to have to think up some way in which to force his hand.

She had a bright smile on her face when Holt came to call for her. And she greeted him with a cheerfulness that hid her thoughts. 'On time, as usual,' she chirruped, and pulled out of arms that might have stayed around her longer, when his greeting was a kiss to her mouth.

'With you at the end of my journey, I broke all speed records,' he teased, and she smiled, and they went out to his car.

Holt took her to a new and well-publicised restaurant, but whose cuisine did not live up to its advertising. But though she noticed that there was quite some of his meal that went untouched, she was glad that the harassed-looking waiter did not come in for the sharp edge of Holt's tongue. And she could only love him more that when she knew Holt was more than capable of sorting out the whole management, that when not lingering, they left the restaurant, his only reference to the meal was to her as he settled her in his car.

'Fancy coming home for beans on toast?'

He'd meant it as a joke, and her mouth did turn up in the amusement they shared. But suddenly she heard herself say, and wish she hadn't:

'Come to think of it, you were going to show me over your home, but you haven't.'

Holt had started the car and was heading it in the direction of Lower Bassett, before he replied, 'You're not so naïve that you haven't figured out the reason for that, are you?'

For one heart-thumping moment, she knew cold shock that from the start he had known she was playing him at his own game. But shock departed when she was unable to see how he could know because even her father, who had met Holt a couple of times on matter concerning business recently, didn't know. She stalled for time.

'I'm sorry, Holt, I'm afraid I must be—I just can't

think of any reason.' Apart, she thought silently, from the fact that since there's not the smallest likelihood of my ever living in your home, there's no point in my looking over it.

'You're saying you've forgotten what happened the first and last time I took you there?' he enquired a touch laconically.

'The night we got en . . Oh!' she exclaimed.

'Exactly,' he replied, and needed to add nothing more.

Though he had given her more than enough to think about during that drive to her home. If she had got it right, Holt was not sure he would not again be making love to her, full and complete love to her, if they should again be isolated in his home.

Though the fact that, when he was playing out this charade like a master, it appeared he still had enough integrity left to remember her saying she didn't think she would be able to look her father in the eye afterwards, brought the pucker of a frown to her forehead.

But by the time he had pulled up outside her home, Verity had forgotten that he had any integrity at all. For a new idea had come to her, and for all of the last five minutes of that drive, while Holt was silent and seemed preoccupied with his own thoughts, she had set her mind to working her idea through.

The main fact, and basis for her idea, was the feeling that was growing and growing in her that with her nerves getting so jumpy, not to mention the depression that closed in on her at times, she didn't know for how much longer she could wait for Holt to have his say. But it appeared Holt was not risking to be alone with her anywhere where a kiss might get out of hand and, desire ruling him, where he might so far forget himself that, when he had no intention whatsoever of marrying her, led by desire, he would—from the way her father would look at it—dishonour her.

It seemed to her that here was an opportunity to put that famous integrity, valued in Holt so highly by her father, to the test.

'I can't promise beans on toast,' she smiled as Holt assisted her from the car at Birchwood House. 'But you'll come in for a coffee, I hope, before you go home.'

His answer was to tuck his hand under her arm and lead her up the steps to her front door. Verity had no thought to tell him that Trudy was visiting friends and was staying overnight. Nor, unless he asked, was she going to tell him that her father was out too. The way she saw it, risky though it was, Holt either had to put his precious integrity in jeopardy by making her his; or, having reached that point of taking her, if his integrity was all her father said it was, he was going to have to be the one to call a halt, and tell her exactly the reason why.

Owning to feeling decidedly shaky inside, she led the way into the drawing room, and invited Holt to take a seat.

'Come and sit with me,' he in turn invited, her idea going swimmingly, she thought, when he caught hold of her hand and pulled her over to the settee. 'I've been very busy of late,' he said with a smiling look at her innocent face, 'but it's all been a means to an end.'

Aware that her nerves were starting to act up, Verity blessed him that when she would have liked in the past to hear all about his work, he had chosen a time such as now to want to discuss it for the first time. But returning his smile, she sat down next to him.

Though when she moved to straighten the skirt of her dress that decorous inch, 'accidentally' she allowed her cheek to brush up against his. And casually, when his face moved against hers, did she turn her head.

Magic, she thought, when just as though there was some homing device on her mouth, Holt too turned, and his lips met hers. But this was one time that when he went to draw back, instead of—in fear of her own response—allowing him so to do, Verity moved her hands up and over his shoulders, an open invitation that she wanted to be kissed again in her eyes.

Holt stilled, his glance going from her eyes to where that invitation was repeated in her parted lips. 'This last month has been the same gruelling hell of wanting for you too?' he enquired softly, dragging his eyes from her mouth and back to the warm brown of her eyes.

'It has been—hell,' she admitted. And, lowering her eyes so he should not see the sudden pain that speared her, 'I don't think I can take—much more.'

'My dear,' he breathed, and there was such pleasure in him at her admission that Verity was fighting that pain and wanting to hate him again that he could find such satisfaction in his aim to make her pay.

But she was soon to be assaulted by other emotions, for just as if there was a sensitivity in him to her needs, Holt had once more placed his mouth tenderly over hers. And as his grip on her tightened, only just could she recall why, on this occasion, she had no intention of pulling out of his arms. For all too soon, as she clung as tightly on to him, was she finding it harder and harder to remember why she had instigated his lovemaking.

But she was having to make herself remember when Holt would have drawn away. And then it was that her lips were seeking and finding his, until, as a groan of wanting left him, he moved her to lie on the settee, his body over hers, as he took up the invitation she was offering.

Though Holt was soon making a nonsense of her memory when she felt the tingle of his tongue, his mouth warm, at the crimson-topped hills of her naked breasts. And she wasn't thinking at all when, no pretence in her at that moment, she arched her body to press against him, aaware of nothing but his need of her, and her need of him.

But suddenly, to cause her more pain. Pain of her own making. Pain which she had brought on herself in her wish to force from him the admission that he had no intention of marrying her, Holt had shot from her as suddenly as she had shot from him that night at his home.

She did not know then, as memory returned, which she hated more—Holt, with his wretched integrity that went so deep it could stay with him when she'd had no thought for integrity or anything else—or if she hated herself that, knowing all there was to know, she could still not prevent his kisses from having that effect on her.

But he was the one to head her hate list when, to show that he still wanted her, wretched integrity or not, his voice had a fiery gritty tone to it when, his eyes seeming unable to move from the creamy swell of her breasts, he barked:

'Cover yourself up, for God's sake!'

Rapidly Verity plummeted to earth. Though it was with shaky fingers that she righted her clothing. She knew what was coming, and she sat up and fought to find the composure she was going to need when he told her what now he had to tell her. Pride demanded that no one saw her in tears—she'd be damned if she'd let him see her cry when he asked for his ring back.

She was still desperately trying to remember the phrase which she had rehearsed and rehearsed ready to come back with when this moment arrived. But she found she still could not remember a word of it, when Holt went and sat in a nearby chair, and muttered:

'I should never have let myself become diverted from what I meant to say, what I had started to say, when we first came in.'

More of her memory arrived, though not memory of the phrase she had been seeking. But sufficient for her to have some faint recall that after asking her to sit with him, Holt had said something about his busy time at work just lately being all a means to an end.

'Th-things did—get a little—er—out of hand, didn't they,' she mumbled, accepting that Holt was going a funny way around it to tell her what he had to tell her, it seeming more important to her then that she worked to ensure that her pride ended up in one piece, aware as she was that there would be no living with herself if she crumpled up before him.

'You can say that again,' he said, a semblance of a smile in his voice which was to give her pride the boost it needed.

Though oddly, she was to feel disappointed in him again, though why she should she couldn't think, because it had always been on the cards that he would gloat when this moment came.

'But,' he went on, 'we won't have to put up with this constant stifling of our emotions for very much longer.'

To Verity's mind it would only take a couple of minutes more before Holt revealed his true colours. But, 'Oh?' she enquired, stamping hard on the desire to beat him to it.

To see him grin at her enquiry brought the anger she sorely required to her aid. The *swine*, the *rat*, she fumed. Not ten minutes ago he was as eager as she in his passion, and yet here he was now, positively gloating in his triumph!

It was a near thing then as her anger pushed for release, that she didn't let go with her anger. But suddenly, anger and all other emotion left her, and she was staring at Holt dumbstruck and just not feeling at all, when with a smile still on his mouth, what he had to say next shattered her completely.

'Thank goodness, the hard toil of these last weeks has paid off,' he said, and his smile broadening, 'And I can now, without having to concern myself over business interests, take you away on our honeymoon.'

Verity was never sure for how long she just sat and stared while what he had just said whirled and whirled around in her head. But when she was able to find enough strength to have any voice, for all her voice was cracked and strangled, she had managed to stutter:

'H-Honeymoon?'

'You seem surprised,' said Holt, a frown replacing his smile. 'I thought you'd understood that I didn't want to wait longer than it took to get my business affairs attended to.'

The only thing that Verity understood then, as cold ice began to encase her, was that there was no end to the lengths he would go to obtain his pound of flesh. And never was she put to having to concentrate more, when, that frown still on his face, Holt asked:

'It *is* all right with you if we marry at the end of this week?'

Had he been halfway to being as sincere as he looked, as he sounded, then Verity knew she would have thrilled to what he was suggesting. 'Of course it is,' she answered. And pride even pushed a smile there, as she apologised for not jumping at his offer. 'I'm sorry,' she said, 'I think I must still be a little confused from—mmm—before.'

'Our lovemaking, you mean?'

She found another smile. 'I'm not so used to—to—er—making love like that, that I can so easily . . .'

She didn't have to finish, for with his frown disappearing, Holt had left his chair and had come to sit beside her. 'Poor darling,' he murmured, placing an arm about her. And with a teasing note, 'It wasn't easy for me either, believe me.' But he was all serious when he said, 'While I'm glad your father saw fit not to disturb us in those minutes you found so confusing, I'm afraid I shall have to disturb him to tell him our plans. Is he in his study?'

'He's out tonight,' she had to confess. But she had no need to feel uncomfortable, that was, if she was capable of feeling anything at all but shock, for Holt took her confession in his stride.

'No matter,' he replied, 'I'll make a point of seeing him some time tomorrow.'

Verity went to bed that night, too shaken by what had happened to be capable of thinking, or even feeling. But that numbness that had taken her to know that Holt wanted his eye for an eye, his tooth for a tooth, so much that he could even plan a wedding date with no intention of being there, was to have worn off by the time she had awakened the next morning. And by that time an ice-cold anger had taken charge of her.

That anger she was to live with was worse than any fury of hot rage which she had ever experienced. But it was that ice-cold anger that was to stay and carry her through the next few days. That ice of anger that encased not just her heart, but every part of her, was to harden whenever she thought of Holt, and how, in revenge for the way she would have assassinated his character had her plan to oust him gone as it should, he was prepared to let her present herself, in a wedding dress, at the church.

That he could allow things to go so far—he'd even

seen her father as he had said he would—appalled her. But since no word of love had come from Holt—not that she had expected it to—it just endorsed for her that when it came to evening up the scores, Holt Jepherson gave no quarter.

Though with her father informed, and obviously expecting her to make some preparation for her wedding, Verity went through the motions of buying a white dress. It was a short dress because, as she explained to him, with the wedding taking place at such short notice and in consequence being a small affair, she thought a long dress would be inappropriate.

But while she could smile and pretend for her father and Trudy that all was right with her world, Verity was aware of that ice in her growing denser and denser each time she thought of Holt. And she just knew that she could not trust her smile to hold up when face to face with him.

It was for that reason that she invented having masses to do in preparation for their wedding, and since Holt would have her believe that he still had a few ends to tidy up before he took her away on a two-month-long honeymoon, she was glad he accepted her excuses that she didn't know when she would find a minute to see him before their wedding day.

But if when he rang each evening she nursed some faint secret hope that this would be the telephone call that would have him saying, 'Don't bother with the white dress,' then not so much as a hint did he give her that she could dress up in her old jeans on Friday for all he would be there to notice.

The stubbornness in Verity that said that she was not going to be the first to call it off had set into a concrete block by Thursday, the eve of the wedding.

'Are you all right?' Holt asked when he rang that

evening, obviously having picked up something of the chill in her that, at this late stage, he was still talking as though he would be there at the church tomorrow.

'I'm fine,' she replied. 'I've been busy, of . . .'

'You're—sure?' he pressed. 'If . . .'

'I'm fine,' she interrupted. And forcing a light laugh when she did not feel she had another laugh in her, 'It's—it's just bridal nerves, I expect.'

Now, she thought, *now*, if that concern she heard in his voice was anything but the phoney concern she knew it for, *now* he would tell her. But his concern *was* phoney, and it was *still* there, though how he could make his voice take on that understanding note, was past her knowing, for after a lengthy pause, it was understandingly that he instructed:

'Don't be scared, Verity. It will be all right, my dear, I promise you.'

She came the nearest to tears then since he had announced their wedding date. But she was still determined not to cry when she came away from the phone with his promise that everything would be all right still ringing in her ears.

By morning that fracture that had looked to be appearing in the ice that cocooned her had been mended. Though she had to own to another weak moment when a smiling Trudy brought her breakfast in bed.

But having survived that moment, Verity was again to feel the sting of tears when Trudy, who had a way with flowers and who was aware that she didn't intend to carry a bouquet, brought her the sweetest little posy, which must have taken her hours to arrange.

'Thank you, Trudy,' she managed, but she was choked, and she had to turn from her.

The ceremony had been arranged for eleven, and it was a quarter to the hour when—with still no last-minute word coming from Holt—aware that her father would be there in a moment to take her the few minutes' drive to the village church, the ice in Verity that had been weakened by Trudy's kindness began to fracture.

The pain started to bite as she sat at her dressing table in her sham of a wedding dress and stared at her pale set face. And then suddenly, she was hurting with an agony of hurt such as she had never known. And all at once, the arctic cold ice that had been with her in her every action this past few days was beginning to crack, and she could do nothing to stop its rapid thaw.

At that very moment her father arrived, to ask, 'Ready, darling?'

Mutely Verity looked to him, the hurt in her a searing pain. She wanted his help, anybody's help, to take the pain away, but she didn't feel like his little girl any longer. For the pain she was feeling was a grown woman's pain, and was not something he could kiss and make better.

'Nervous?' he asked, reading totally wrongly the never-before-seen haunted look in her eyes. 'That's not like you, love,' he teased gently. Then, 'Shall we go? I know it's usual to be late, but . . .'

'I'm—not coming.'

'What—did you say?' asked Clement Diamond, as though sure he had misheard her.

'I said . . .' replied Verity, '. . . that I have no intention of—marrying Holt Jepherson.'

'You've just *got* to be joking!'

She shook her head to tell him that this was no joke. Then she saw his expression slowly change. Then, while her inside was screaming with her hurt, he asked why, and when she could not answer, she was made to sit and listen while first he tried to coax; and when that did no good, he tried to order; and when that did no good either, she had to sit with her heart breaking into small fragmented pieces, and listen while he set off on an enraged tirade that lasted all of five minutes, but which he could see had made not the slightest difference to her decision.

'My God!' he roared then, 'I'll make damn sure this is the last stunt you'll ever pull! Just you wait right there—there're a few things I shall have to say to you when I get back!'

But by then, even though she knew that he would have a wasted journey if he was going to the church to tell Holt that it was all off, the hurt in her had reached too much of a pitch for her to speak. And the tears which she had fought so hard not to shed would just not be kept at bay any longer.

Great convulsive sobs racked her as she wept those bitter salt tears. Tears, which this time there was no controlling, drenched her eyes. Even as she was aware that no amount of crying would heal her broken heart, she wept on and was unable to stop those tears from falling.

For how long she gave way, as the ice in her melted into tears, she was beyond knowing. But when she was oblivious to anything but that hurt that was ripping her apart, suddenly, to penetrate that crippling pain, came the sound of a car hurtling up the drive at speed.

Her first thought was that it was her father who, forgetting his stern lectures on the way she had driven on a couple of occasions, had come roaring back to ask to be forgiven for all the harsh things he had said to her.

But, when the engine cut, and Verity heard the sound of sprinting footsteps that had far more energy to them than her father's portly body would allow, as her proud hand instinctively went for a tissue to mop up her tear-washed face and eyes—her thoughts began hopping all over the place!

CHAPTER ELEVEN

HER hopping thoughts were still jumping about looking for a place to land, when Verity heard those energetic footsteps come bounding up the stairs. But that neither her father nor Trudy ever went in for charging up the stairs like that was about all she had time to realise. For while her brain went numb, and even her heart seemed to cease to beat, she heard that those striding footsteps were making for her room.

Her eyes became transfixed on the door. And suddenly that door was thrust open—and Holt Jepherson filled the doorway. It was then that her heart started to beat again. Rapid, hurried, racing beats, to make her breath catch, her eyes growing enormous when she saw from his pristine white shirt, from his dark suit—complete with buttonhole—that she had been very much mistaken to think that Holt would not put in an appearance at the church.

But that was not all Verity observed about him. The way that the door had been thrown nearly off its hinges had told her that he wasn't very pleased about something, but the longer he stood staring at her with hostile eyes, the more chance did she have to note that besides having lost some of his normal colour in his fury, Holt was in a barely controlled blistering rage.

It was all there in the dangerously quiet way he said, 'I *knew* it! Even when I was telling myself I was mistaken, I just knew things were going far too smoothly for you not to be up to something.'

He knew that *she* was up to something! God, did he have a nerve! Verity welcomed the heat of anger that, for the first time in days, was suddenly sparked into life. That welcome anger was there to have her ignore that Holt looked to be enraged enough to toss her out of the first-floor window if she gave him any lip.

'Well, now you know,' she said, uncaring that his eyes had narrowed ominously.

'So I do,' he agreed grimly. 'Which leaves me giving you two choices.'

'Generous to a fault, I see,' said Verity, the fight in her that had seen her surrendering to tears not long since coming to join anger; both refusing to step down in the face of his hands clenching and unclenching menacingly down at his sides, as, 'What magnanimous choice do you think I might so much as *consider* taking from you?' she asked snappily.

The working of his jaw told her she was pushing it. But in telling herself that that didn't worry her, she was utterly flabbergasted when he replied tightly:

'Just this. Do you come to that church voluntarily, or do I carry you there?'

That he could think she would put one foot inside that church had her jaw dropping. But she was speechless for only two seconds.

'Neither!' she flew. 'And don't you try to use caveman tactics on me!' she yelled, instinctively backing when it looked as if he was going to come and get her. But panic of the moment taking from her mind all thought that he had no intention of marrying her anyway, 'I won't marry you if you drag me down that aisle by the roots of my hair,' she told him.

'You will,' he contradicted her shortly, the furious glint in his eyes confirming that, despite his quiet tone, Holt was inwardly raging. 'No one breaks a promise to me, Verity Diamond,' he added, 'and that includes you.'

'What,' she scoffed, 'when I hate you worse than poison?'

Something seemed to snap in Holt then. She rather thought it was his control on his anger. For in a stride he had moved from the doorway and had snatched up the beautiful posy Trudy had made for her. Then at the same moment of pushing the posy into her hands, he had hauled her to her feet.

'Hate away,' he snarled, 'but marry me you will!'

'Like hell I will!' Verity yelled in panic, throwing the posy to the bed so she should have both hands free to push at his chest.

'You're dressed for it,' he gritted, refusing to be pushed from her, his grip firming to be two iron bands on her upper arms.

'So are you,' she cried, tears of frustration flooding her eyes as she saw that with his superior strength he could have her at that church with curious-eyed villagers having a heyday as the two of them fought it out all the way down the aisle. 'But that doesn't mean . . .'

'Tears!' Suddenly, although she had tried to hide the shine in her eyes, Holt had witnessed it. Some of his mighty fury seemed to ebb then, and if before he had been consumed with rage that he had been oblivious to her reddened eyes, close up to her with some of his anger gone, he was observing, and accusing, 'You've been crying!'

'What if I have?' she snapped, pride lifting her straight away up on to her high horse.

'Why?' he demanded, an alert look in his eyes which she would have preferred had not been there.

'Why not?' she answered carelessly. But she might have guessed he would not leave it there.

'Why, because you're not the crying type. Why, because you, with your mammoth pride, would think it beneath you to give way to your feelings and weep like ordinary mortals. Why, because you think yourself too much of a tough nut to let anything get on top of you to cause you tears.'

'How lovely you make me sound!' she shot at him, just to let him know that she didn't care *that* much for his opinion.

'But you are lovely,' he replied without making it sound like a compliment. 'You have a wealth of pride, and beauty too. But there's so much of you, Verity Diamond, that's all so much sham—all so much on the surface.'

He cut through her sarcastic, 'Do tell me more.'

'Under that careless, anything-for-a-laugh exterior you show the world lies a warm and sensitive being. You're a woman with a soft heart, capable of deep feeling. A woman who'll put her father before her own . . .'

'I hardly recognise myself,' Verity cut in acidly, the reminder that initially, it had been for her father's sake that she would have gone through with a marriage to Holt—had his offer been anything but a set-up—most timely.

'I recognise you,' he said shortly. 'Just as I recognise that something must have affected you pretty deeply that, albeit in secret, you've given way to tears.'

Verity was not caring very much for the insight Holt had into her character; for his insight into what made her tick. And she was panicking again as all at once it struck her that if he knew so much about her, if he pushed that little bit harder, it could be he would discover what a liar she had been too when she had told him she hated him.

'Quite obviously,' she said, adopting an airy tone that was vastly at odds with the way she was feeling, 'you've never heard of tears of joy, of—of tears of delight . . .'

'You're saying you were crying from joy!' he exclaimed, astounded. But his anger was on the rampage again, she felt it in the way his hands clenched on her arms, even before, still sounding stunned, he asked angrily, 'You're saying that to think you'd made a fool of me gave you such joy that you wept tears of delight!'

'*Me*—made a fool of *you*!' she exclaimed, never one to have one put over on her either. 'My God, you've got a . . .' she had halted, but as the real reason for his fury suddenly hit her, she did not pause for long. And fury was in her too as she positively hurled at him, 'The only reason you're here now is because you can't take it that I've deprived you of the pleasure *you* wanted at making a *fool* of me!'

'You thought . . .!' It was quite something for her to see Holt for once speechless. But like her, he was not speechless for long. 'What crazy idea have you . . .'

'Oh, cut out the pretence, Holt,' she stormed, 'it was never on anyway. I've known what you were up to since way back. The only thing I didn't know was how far you would go before . . .'

'What the hell are you talking about?' he cut her off. But his look of being mystified did not deceive her for a second.

'You know damn well what I'm talking about,' she retorted angrily. And with another push at his chest proving equally unrewarding, the belligerence in her was let loose with a vengeance, as frustrated and furious, she yelled, 'What was your plan, to wait until I'd got my "I will" said, before you burst out laughing?'

'For God's sake,' Holt roared, making tears sting her eyes that he was *still* hell bent on playing it to the limit, when he just had to know she had seen through him, 'will you talk in a language I can understand!'

'You're saying you don't know what I'm talking about,' she scorned. But she very nearly had her eardrums shattered, as when, that close she would have heard him had he whispered, Holt fairly bellowed in his exasperation:

'Would I bloody well ask if I did?'

She jumped at the violent aggression in him. But she had soon recovered to scoff, 'Huh! You're a clever man, Holt, sharper than most. Are you trying to tell me that having spoken to my father, you haven't been able to put two and two together?'

'I've spoken with him many times,' he told her tersely. 'About business, as well as having a word with him when we became engaged. But none of what we spoke of,' he went on grittily, 'was to give me as much as a hint that when I arrived in church, I would find that not only would you customarily be late, but that Clement should come alone and tell me you didn't intend to come at all.'

From that angry speech, Verity knew that as well as keeping his promise not to tell Holt that she loved him, her father had kept the other part of his promise too, and had not told Holt that she was aware of their original plan to give her the fright of her life. But her father wasn't low on the grey matter either, and he should, to her mind, have been able to reason and to give Holt a clue, for all he had been breathing fire when he'd left her, as to what lay at the root of her refusal to budge.

'You're saying that my father didn't tell you why I wasn't coming?' she challenged. For her trouble, her ears were again made to ring.

'Dammit, woman!' Holt thundered. 'Your father's as much in the dark as I am!'

Oh, how convincing he sounded. It made Verity madder than ever that even now he was still playing it for all he was worth.

'Then you both want locking up!' she shouted. And with the strength of ten in her fury, she wrenched herself out of his hold and went to stand several yards away from him, her eyes flashing out signals of fury, that told of her shot control.

She thought Holt was going to come after her, but his movement to do so was suddenly arrested, and she wasn't sure then that he did not look to be a shade disappointed in her, when:

'Good God,' he breathed, 'so *that's* what all this is about!'

She was certain she didn't care a damn how disappointed in her Holt was. Though it wasn't so much disappointment in her, she started to see, but more disappointment that she had fouled up his plans to have the best laugh yet—and at her expense.

'It's clicked, has it?' she asked sourly.

'If you mean have I only realised that you're so vindictive that I have your seat on the board, that you'll stop at nothing to make me suffer for it, then yes, it's clicked,' said Holt grimly. And when, wide-eyed at what he had said, she just stared, he was to astonish her further, when he added, 'Well, if you want that seat so much, I'll make you a wedding present of it.' And he had not finished astounding her yet, for while her thoughts went on a second hopping trip, he had mastered whatever emotion was going on in him and was saying, 'Now, are you coming to that church voluntarily, or am I going to carry you?'

Quite clearly then, she gained the impression that now she had got what she had been after, he thought he would not have to carry her anywhere, and that she would be charging down that aisle in front of him in her eagerness to claim her wedding gift.

'J-Just a minute,' she stammered, when he moved as though expecting her to move too.

'There's something I've missed?' he asked, his voice coldly sceptical, as he checked his step to the door.

'Quite a lot, actually,' she replied, uncertain how she suddenly came to be on the defensive, though owning that perhaps it was the shock of what he had said that had put her there.

But when Holt waited, and said not another word, it was the hostile expression with which he stood favouring her that gave her enough of a spark to tell him, her face as unsmiling as his:

'For the record, Jepherson, that seat on the board is no longer among my list of priorities.'

She had thought him sceptical before, but sceptical didn't begin to cover the disbelieving way in which he replied, 'Isn't it?'

'Damn you!' she flared, in sudden anger slipping up and revealing the truth of her thinking these past weeks. 'You'd make a better board member than me, and you know it!'

She looked away from him, realising then, when that alert look sped into his eyes, that her flare of anger had seen her saying more than she had meant to say. Nor was she any happier in that, his scepticism starting to fade, Holt was still showing himself smarter than her, in that he had quickly sifted through her previous statement and had thought to ask:

'If that seat no longer heads your lists of priorities, might one be allowed to know what came along to push it from top place?'

She had no answer. None that she was going to give him, anyway. 'Oh, shut up,' she said irritably, back on the defensive again and not liking it very much.

'Ah,' said Holt, which told her nothing, save that from the way he had said it, he had not taken exception to her telling him to shut up. 'What are you trying to hide, Verity?' he asked mildly, too mildly for him.

Alarm surged through her then as quickly, perhaps too quickly, she replied, 'Nothing. I'm hiding nothing.' Holt was shaking his head, even before she had finished.

'You are,' he disagreed. 'You know it, and I know it. Just as I know that whatever it is, it has something to do with you thinking to pay me out by not turning up at that church—which in turn means that it has to have something to do with me.'

There was no thought in Verity of folding, but since from the set look of him, Holt was going to go on picking and picking away until he got at the truth, and as it was of paramount importance to her pride that he should never know how heart and soul in love with him she was, there seemed nothing for it but to come clean on what he would insist on knowing anyway.

'It wasn't a question of paying you out,' she said after an inner struggle. 'I've known almost from the very beginning that you never had any intention of marrying me. I just didn't fancy going along to that church only to . . .'

'You thought I had no intention of marrying you?' Holt exclaimed, thunderstruck. Though his aggression was not very far behind. 'What the hell do you think I'm doing here now if I'm supposed to be playing some weird kind of hoax on you?' he demanded.

'You—I didn't expect—you to turn up,' she said, the sudden lurch of her heart, the thudding in her head, all there to make her speech hesitant. But as she stared at him and saw that he looked ready to explode in exasperation at her answer, she saw he looked to be doing his best not to lose patience and come slamming into her.

'Have I,' he asked, his voice quiet with control, 'ever given you any reason to think I wouldn't be there this morning?'

'Yes,' she replied. And before he could ask the sharp 'When?' which she saw was coming, quickly she was there to tell him how her father had revealed the way in which they had thought to frighten the life out of her. Though her voice had started to trail off when she saw that Holt was looking absolutely incredulous, as, 'So I knew when you put this engagement ring on my finger,' belatedly, she removed it, 'that you were only paying me back for what I did to you.'

'My—God!' It was all Holt seemed to be capable of to breathe for several stunned seconds. Then he was recovering to ask, 'You actually believed, *all this time*, that I was so set on having my revenge that I would go so far as to let you arrive in church on your wedding day . . .' he seemed to be having a hard time taking it in. 'You believed I thought so little of you that I could dishonour you in such a way?'

Her heart had ceased to merely thud. At that intimation that he did think a little of her, her heart had picked up speed and had begun to race. Even while she knew that if Holt was meaning that he did think something of her, and that meant that there was a long way to go before it could mean that he loved her a little, her racing heart still refused to behave.

'What else—was I to think?' she mumbled. Only for her heart to go leaping wildly, when he told her quietly:

'I stopped playing games with you, Verity, on the night I put that engagement ring on your finger.'

Scarcely able to draw breath then, Verity was suddenly to remember how her father had been convinced that Holt would not give her an engagement ring unless he had meant to marry her.

'You stopped . . .' she echoed on a gasp, but it was all she had breath for.

'I didn't come clean about that plot I had conjured

up with your father's connivance,' Holt, his eyes watchful on her, went on when nothing else was coming from her, 'because, believing you still in the dark, I couldn't risk you saying that in that case you saw no reason why you should marry me.'

All the saliva in her mouth dried at his words. But even though her throat felt parched, she just had to ask a choky:

'You—sound—as though you—want—to marry me?'

A muscle jerked in his temple, but it was only a moment before, quite clearly, she heard him say, 'I do.' Then quickly, as if to deny her the right of refusal, he was turning to the door, and adding, 'We're late now, but the vicar will wait if we . . .'

'No.'

Her voice had stopped him, and had him turning back to face her. But when everything about him spoke of control, Verity heard that his voice was not so even, when he asked:

'Are you saying that with everything now clear between us, now you know for sure that you don't have to go through with it for your father's sake, you will not marry me?'

'No, I'm not saying that,' she said hurriedly, hardly daring to believe that it was relief she saw briefly in his face. 'It's just that—that—I find it hard to b-believe that—when you thought I was capable of being so vindictive that I would—well, I just c-can't see why you should want to—to marry me.'

Holt hesitated, and seemed impatient, in a hurry, and as though he would tell her that it did not matter now, but that she should just accept things as they stood. But while most of Verity wanted to do just that, even while she wanted to snatch at what chance she had with Holt, and with both hands, that stubborn streak in her that could be the means of him becoming fed up, and telling her, 'Forget it,' had her not budging until she knew why, when he could marry just about anybody he chose, he should want to marry her.

'You have my word,' he said at last, 'that I'm sincere in my wish to marry you. That I have every intention of joining with you in making our marriage vows today. You must believe me,' he went on, 'when I tell you that I will not, and could not ever, make you the laughing stock you envisaged I would make of you in church this morning.'

'I do believe you, Holt,' said Verity quietly, and believe him she did. Indeed, it seemed impossible to her then that she had ever thought him less than sincere. But that still did not answer her question. 'I know,' she said, choosing her words carefully, 'that perhaps I've been a—a tiny bit of a hell-raiser in the past, and that maybe you haven't heard or seen anything in me to make you think you can trust me. But—but I would—dearly like you to trust me now, Holt, and . . . and tell me why? Why it's me that you want to marry? I mean,' she had to pause to swallow, but she had to go pressing on with what was the most difficult speech of her whole life, 'I'm aware that, physically, everything happens when—when . . .'

'When we get together,' he inserted quietly, seeing that she needed some assistance.

Verity nodded. 'But it has to be something more than that, doesn't it?'

'It does,' he agreed solemnly, but his knuckles were suddenly showing white when, his voice still quiet, he said, 'And it is.'

Pink colour flushed her cheeks. She felt breathless again, and as though she had just sprinted a mile. 'You're saying that . . .' She just couldn't finish, her nerve had run out.

But, having come this far, Holt took a deep breath, and stepped across the room to take hold of her hands. But, while her heart was hammering as if it would take off, he did not at once speak, but paused to dismay her for a moment by taking the engagement ring from her clutched fingers, to place it on her third finger of her right hand. Then, while her heart was doing a rapid slide to her boots that he must in effect be saying the 'Forget it' she had been afraid of, and that he must also be saying that their engagement was off, but that she could keep the ring, he told her evenly:

'You can return that ring to your left hand as soon as I've placed a gold band there.' Her heart rocketing upwards again, Holt's voice was controlled when he said, 'I want to marry you, and have known that I will marry you and no other, ever since that day when, a guest in this house, you came to my room and belligerently said "Word has it that you want to marry me".'

'But you didn't,' Verity argued. 'You said you would marry me,' she remembered. 'But you definitely said that you didn't *want* to . . .' she broke off, confused. And Holt, seeing her confusion owned:

'What else was I to say? I'd just been knocked for six to realise what all the signs I'd been set on ignoring had just added up to.'

'Signs?' she repeated, suddenly on an up-down see-saw and not sure that her powers of comprehension were standing up to being as good as she had always thought them any more. 'Er—what signs?' she asked.

Holt still had hold of her hands, but when a minute ago he had been in a rush to get her out through the door, minutes seemed to have ticked by before he said:

'Signs such as feeling so irked when a beautiful girl I'd already noticed at a certain country club—a girl I didn't know from Eve, and who normally would have had me cutting her down to size when she was so pointedly rude to me—had me going after her to the car park to find out what the hell it was I was supposed to have done.'

Verity wasn't so sure that she wanted to be reminded of her appalling rudeness that night. 'You—er—gave me a lift home,' she murmured in some sort of an apology, though the way she remembered it, she hadn't had any choice but to accept that lift.

'And telephoned you the next day, and called here to see you, without having the first idea why I should. A personal visit, or a phone call, was necessary.'

'You said . . .' she started off, then found that what with her heart banging away as if to crack her ribs, and what with Holt's hands still nursing hers, that what he had said then was somewhat cloudy in her brain. 'You seemed,' she started off again, 'when you called here that time, to be most concerned that my father works so hard.'

'Your father,' said Holt, his grey eyes fixed on hers, 'is a man who thrives on hard work.'

'Oh,' she said. But she had to swallow hard before she could ask, 'Are y-you saying that you made your concern that he should rest an—an excuse for—for calling—that time?'

'In those early days of knowing you, my dear,' he replied, 'there was no end to the excuses I found for this need I discovered I have to—be near to you.'

Pink was again to riot in her face. But, wanting so much to believe what she was hearing, Verity was too afraid that she had it wrong to be able to utter a sound.

'There was no reason whatsoever why I couldn't have driven back to Drake's Knighton on the night your father and I had some business to talk over,' Holt went on when she could not find her tongue. 'But with my need to be near you, unrecognised then, I accepted his invitation. Though only to discover you wouldn't be in to dinner, and for me to go to bed that night and find that I couldn't sleep a wink until you came home. And when eventually I did hear you come home, I was to lie awake wondering if you'd been daft enough to get engaged to that chap Robey.'

An excitement wanted to well up in Verity, but she was still afraid she might have got it all wrong. And afraid as she was to give a hint of how it was with her, all she managed to get out was a fractured-sounding:

'You—said you were a-awake when I—er—came to your room.'

'I was,' replied Holt. 'I was awake, and feeling never less like reading, when you came in and joined me. It seemed light years until Mrs Trueman arrived.' A warm note had entered his voice when he said, 'And then I kissed you, and it was when I kissed you that a new and different excitement took me—I'd never felt so alive in my life as when I held you in my arms,' he murmured. 'It was then that I knew I was on the brink of something.'

'You d-didn't know then,' she gulped, 'w-what it was?'

Holt's hands, leaving hers and coming up to hold her gently by the shoulders, had her striving hard not to show that she was needing to swallow again. But she was gripping on to the sides of him for all she was worth, when, his eyes never leaving hers, he shook his head.

'No, I didn't know then,' he agreed. 'Not until after I'd tried to make light of you climbing into my bed to your father—and seen him near to a stroke in his rage with you—did I know. But it was there to shake my very foundations when, up in my room, in the middle of telling you that I'd never stated that I wanted to marry you, I was suddenly rocked to realise that yes, by God, I did want to marry you—and why.'

Her fingers were positively digging into Holt then. And as if her life depended on it, with every nerve in her body seeming to be jumping, she could not stop the words of desperately wanting to know that reason from leaving her.

'Please, Holt, please tell me why,' she begged.

His hold on her shoulders had been gentle. But at her pleading, his grip tightened into a fierce grip. 'You sound,' he said slowly, 'as though—it could mean something to you?'

Verity choked to get the words out. 'It—could,' she admitted honestly.

'Are you saying,' it was Holt who swallowed then before he could continue, 'that you, Verity Diamond, have—a quarter—of the love for me that I hold in my heart for you?'

Tears she could not check, and did not wish to check, rushed to her eyes. And while Holt looked more than a little disturbed to see those tears spill over and tumble one after the other down her cheeks, she struggled, and finally managed to get out the words:

'Oh, Holt Jepherson, I love you. I *love you!*'

She had never thought to see Holt look so stunned, or to hear his voice so hoarse when, 'It's the truth, Verity?' he asked. 'For God's sake tell me it's the truth and that you aren't . . .'

'It's the truth,' she butted in as, more tears falling unheeded down her face, she did not wait for him to accuse her of being up to something. 'When you arrived, I was breaking my heart over you, but . . .'

The next moment her head was pressed to his chest, and his arms were tight around her—that she was letting him see the tears fall from her proud eyes was all the endorsement he needed that she was speaking the truth.

His entirely, Verity clung to him, in rapture when he murmured 'Oh, my darling love, I love you so much. Yet with the proof of your love in your tears—I can't bear to see you cry.'

'I can't seem to stop,' she smiled, and she could not.

But she was soon on his lap in the bedroom chair, and her head was on his arm and chest as he cradled her and tenderly mopped up each tear as it fell. And it was with her emotions all over the place that Verity told him:

'Now you know what tears of joy look like.'

He smiled, and bent to kiss her weeping eyes. But success was his in stopping the flow of her tears, when tenderly his mouth settled over hers.

'Oh, Holt,' she breathed, when finally his lips left hers, 'I've loved you for such a long time, it just doesn't seem possible that there isn't any pain in me any more.'

'My beautiful sweetheart,' he murmured, 'I never wanted you to feel hurt.' Then he was kissing every part of her face as if to make sure that every trace of pain was gone from her. And then he was asking, 'When did you know that you felt something for me other than hate?'

'That night, that second night you stayed here,' she answered softly, but without hesitation. 'My father had just washed his hands with me on account of what he calls my reckless driving, and you'd come up to the door of this room with me, and I knew then.'

Holt kissed her, and as if that kiss was not enough, he kissed her again and again, his kisses growing deeper and deeper. And he appeared to have the same difficulty as she did in remembering her last sentence when finally they drew apart. Though smiling his love, he remembered:

'That was the day your poor demented father had

me as demented with worry as him. That was the night,' he kissed her cheek, 'when I had to push you into your room to return to mine and to spend yet another wakeful night wanting you back in my bed again. Which reminds me,' he said, moving her to her feet, but standing close to her, 'am I going to have the right to hold you close to my heart and in my bed tonight?'

'If you're asking me to marry you,' she smiled, confidence in his love growing in her, 'then the answer is yes.'

Holt kissed her lingeringly, his love there in his eyes when at last he looked into her face—then he was pausing only to hand her the posy from the bed, and he was then hurrying her out to his car.

And it was on that short drive to the church that, not wanting any secrets between them, Verity confessed how she had tried to get him to own up to not wanting to marry her, on that night he had suddenly sprung their wedding date on her.

'Allow me to tell you, Miss Diamond,' he replied with a grin, 'that I shall never know from where I found the will power not to give in, and let myself be seduced.' And while she giggled and went only a little pink, Holt in turn was confessing, 'And I was so afraid to tell you of my love for fear of hearing something I didn't want to hear, that as soon as I'd got my work clear I had to spring our wedding date on you in the hope that if I rushed you, you wouldn't have time to think up some good reason to object. I was hoping,' he added softly, 'that once married to you, I could try to earn a little of your love.'

Verity had time only then to send him a look that told him he had all of her love, for they were pulling up outside the church.

She caught sight of her father pacing up and down,

and he came hurrying to them as they walked up the church path. But one look at her radiant face was sufficient to take the worried look from him. Though it was not to her that he addressed his remarks, but to the man whose arm was holding her close by his side as though he never intended to let her go.

'Tell me, Holt,' he said, 'am I losing a daughter?—*Please!*'

Holt grinned as he spared a glance from his love so close to him. 'Verity came willingly—didn't you, darling?' he replied.

'Never more willingly,' she agreed tenderly, and between the man who loved her with a father's love, and the man who loved her as the husband he would shortly be, as willingly as she had said, she went into the church.

The next words she spoke were to make her vows. And tears were again glistening in her eyes when, uncaring who saw them, with those words exchanged that united them as husband and wife, she saw the same heartfelt joy in Holt's proud eyes, as:

'I love you, Verity Jepherson,' he whispered.

Take these 4 best-selling novels FREE

Yes! Four sophisticated, contemporary love stories by four world-famous authors of romance FREE, as your introduction to the Harlequin Presents subscription plan. Thrill to **Anne Mather**'s passionate story BORN OUT OF LOVE, set in the Caribbean.... Travel to darkest Africa in **Violet Winspear**'s TIME OF THE TEMPTRESS....Let **Charlotte Lamb** take you to the fascinating world of London's Fleet Street in MAN'S WORLD .... Discover beautiful Greece in **Sally Wentworth**'s moving romance SAY HELLO TO YESTERDAY.

Harlequin Presents...

The very finest in romance fiction

Join the millions of avid Harlequin readers all over the world who delight in the magic of a really exciting novel. EIGHT great NEW titles published EACH MONTH! Each month you will get to know exciting, interesting, true-to-life people .... You'll be swept to distant lands you've dreamed of visiting .... Intrigue, adventure, romance, and the destiny of many lives will thrill you through each Harlequin Presents novel.

Get all the latest books before they're sold out!

As a Harlequin subscriber you actually receive your personal copies of the latest Presents novels immediately after they come off the press, so you're sure of getting all 8 each month.

Cancel your subscription whenever you wish!

You don't have to buy any minimum number of books. Whenever you decide to stop your subscription just let us know and we'll cancel all further shipments.

Your FREE gift includes

Anne Mather—Born out of Love
Violet Winspear—Time of the Temptress
Charlotte Lamb—Man's World
Sally Wentworth—Say Hello to Yesterday

Mail this coupon today!

FREE Gift Certificate
and subscription reservation

Harlequin Reader Service

In the U.S.A.
2504 West Southern Ave.
Tempe, AZ 85282

In Canada
P.O. Box 2800, Postal Station A
5170 Yonge Street,
Willowdale, Ont. M2N 6J3

Please send me my 4 Harlequin Presents books
free. Also, reserve a subscription to the 8 new
Harlequin Presents novels published each
month. Each month I will receive 8 new Presents
novels at the low price of $1.75 each [*Total—
$14.00 a month*]. There are no shipping and
handling or any other hidden charges. I am free to
cancel at any time, but even if I do, these first 4
books are still mine to keep absolutely FREE
without any obligation. 108 BPP CAGE

NAME _____ (PLEASE PRINT)

ADDRESS _____ APT. NO. _____

CITY _____

STATE/PROV. _____ ZIP/POSTAL CODE _____

This offer is limited to one order per household and not valid to
current *Harlequin Presents* subscribers. We reserve the right
to exercise discretion in granting membership.

® ™ Trademarks of Harlequin Enterprises Ltd.   P-SUB-2US

If price changes are necessary you will be notified.

Just what the woman on the go needs!

BOOKMATE

The perfect "mate" for all Harlequin paperbacks!

Holds paperbacks open for hands-free reading!

- **TRAVELING**
- **VACATIONING**
- **AT WORK • IN BED**
- **COOKING • EATING**
- **STUDYING**

Perfect size for all standard paperbacks, this wonderful invention makes reading a pure pleasure! Ingenious design holds paperback books OPEN and FLAT so even wind can't ruffle pages—leaves your hands free to do other things. Reinforced, wipe-clean vinyl-covered holder flexes to let you turn pages without undoing the strap...supports paperbacks so well, they have the strength of hardcovers!

Snaps closed for easy carrying.

Available now. Send your name, address, and zip or postal code, along with a check or money order for just $4.99 + .75¢ for postage & handling (for a total of $5.74) payable to Harlequin Reader Service to:

Harlequin Reader Service

In the U.S.A.
2504 West Southern Ave.
Tempe, AZ 85282

In Canada
P.O. Box 2800, Postal Station A
5170 Yonge Street,
Willowdale, Ont. M2N 5T5

MATE-1R